Airship Daedalus

Raiders of the Red Storm

By Todd Downing

FIRST EDITION

ISBN: 979-8-9861181-2-3

Copyright © 2021 Todd Downing & Deep7 Press

All Rights Reserved Worldwide

Edited by Andrea Edelman

Sensitivity reader Devielle Johnson

Cover art & design by Todd Downing
(*Daedalus* model by Hans Piwenitzky)

Based on the *Airship Daedalus / AEGIS Tales* setting and characters by Todd Downing and published in various media by Deep7 Press. *Airship Daedalus*™ and *AEGIS Tales*™ are trademarks of Deep7 Press.

WWW.AIRSHIPDAEDALUS.COM

Deep7 Press is a subsidiary of Despot Media, LLC
1214 Woods Rd SE Port Orchard, WA 98366 USA
WWW.DEEP7.COM

PRINTED IN USA

Thanks to E.J. Blaine

for the kernel of this story.

- PRELUDE -

London, April 1929

A single light shone in the third-floor window of the red brick townhouse on Green Street, Mayfair. One solitary, unblinking, rectangular eye, casting its gaze across the lane. The golden beam extended from its source, almost solid in the midnight fog. Gauzy, white curtains were drawn, like a filmy cataract, allowing only shadows and silhouettes to play across its tiny stage.

The hearth in the study was ablaze with a healthy fire, the other light source being a Tiffany table lamp which sat beside an over-stuffed leather armchair. Aleister Crowley sat ensconced there, staring into the dancing firelight. He wore a tartan wool beret on a balding pate, eyes sunken, skin sallow in the flickering firelight. An emerald green velvet smoking jacket contained a body in decline: once a specimen of healthy masculinity, now ravaged by poor diet, drug addiction, and diseases of carnal excess. He was neither plump nor emaciated, his bones merely suspended in a container of atrophied muscle and skin.

The woman sat opposite Crowley, cross-legged on the edge of the maroon crushed velvet sofa. Literally opposite in most every way, from her toned alabaster complexion to her plump, bee-stung lips, and raven-black hair cut in the severe bobbed style that was all the rage in Weimar Germany. She wore a colorful silk kimono which draped her taut frame from neck to mid-calf, bare feet displaying nails the same color as the couch she sat upon. She held a crystal goblet in her left hand, delicately whirling the claret within, staring past the glass toward her patron with furtive blue eyes.

From their state of dress, and the placement of a portable altar and several arcane props and accouterments, it could be easily deduced that the couple had recently finished consummating some sort of sexual magic ritual. And it probably wouldn't be the only ritual executed this night.

They sat in silence, pondering their relationship over the past decade. Maria Gunnhild had been a spy for the Central Powers in the Great War. When Crowley found her in its aftermath, she was emotionally broken and needy, yet single-minded of purpose, a purpose which matched his own: the acquisition of unbridled power, and revenge upon their enemies. It was that drive which appealed to Crowley.

It was the only thing which exempted her from the requirement of the Soul Contract: wherein he could, at any time, summon a follower's life force back to himself, causing the acolyte to disintegrate in a smoldering pile of ash and bone, leaving only clothing and possessions. It worked regardless of geography or circumstance, and it was why precisely zero agents of the *Astrum Argentum*—the Silver Star Society—had ever been captured. Without the Soul Contract hanging over her like a Sword of Damocles, Maria proved herself a star pupil and eventually became a powerful magus in her own right. She took the surname Blutig, meaning "bloody", and became the "She-Wolf of the *Astrum Argentum*."

In their ten years together, Maria had been both at Crowley's right hand and in the doghouse at various times, depending on his mercurial temperament, or how a particular operation had fared. The summoning of the demon Choronzon in the Amazon in 1925 had been thwarted by a small crew of agents working for a foundation of American industrialists. The flagship of Crowley's paramilitary force, a super-zeppelin called *Luftpanzer*, was destroyed, Crowley and Maria each barely escaping with their lives.

The setback had been momentary.

By the following year, a larger, more heavily-armed version of the *Luftpanzer* was deployed to the Himalayas. There, the Silver Star constructed a science base in a thermal valley at the "Eye of the World", where the source of the planet's most potent toxin grew wild. Quickly, an operation was launched, to assassinate the American titans of industry behind the mystery organization—AEGIS, they called it. Latin for "armor" or "shield". Headed by an aging Thomas Edison and manned by former Allied soldiers from the war, they existed only to be a thorn in Crowley's side. At least that was how Crowley saw it, and that was what mattered. Forging an alliance with both federal authorities and organized crime, the AEGIS operatives stopped the assassination program, and tracked the toxin back to its source. In the battle that raged on the ground and in the sky, the outpost was destroyed and the valley sealed off from the outside world.

Another failure.

Maria was assigned to New York on a reconnaissance mission, having fallen from Crowley's favor. Meanwhile the Master commissioned a new super-carrier—an enormous airship called *Osiris*, after the Egyptian death god—and gave command to a Dutch officer named Ernst Hummel. Working with the Dutchman had been a matter of expedience, and their partnership had been largely successful. They'd captured the crew of the AEGIS airship *Percival* on its maiden voyage, and Maria had used their blood in a summoning ritual in an ancient temple to Set, buried in the Egyptian desert. This time, she'd been intent on bringing forth Ammit, the Soul-Eater. But once again, the crew of the airship *Daedalus* had foiled her plans.

Yet, even in the midst of a rear-guard escape, the Silver Star managed to take one of the experimental dynamos powering the AEGIS light recon airships, and the man who was the world's foremost expert in their workings. Maria found herself back in the Master's good graces and commanding a special science mission for a young Heinrich Himmler.

Leading the *Daedalus* and *Percival* on a chase across India, Southeast Asia, and the Pacific expanse, the Silver Star dropped an invasion force on a mysterious island where, decades previous, an English surgeon had performed highly unethical experiments on the native human and animal populations, creating multiple hybrid species. They'd been reproducing over three generations, evolving into a civilized and benevolent society. While Maria led an arcane summoning of spider-like demons from a hellish dimension, Himmler's team trapped them in special electronic storage devices, to be used as a power source in future Silver Star technology.

But when the ritual went wrong and the demons began to escape onto the island, it became clear that the only way to seal the rift was from the other side, and Maria vanished into the fabric of space and time. She was gone over a year, long enough to be presumed dead. It was also long enough for Captain Hummel to be assigned to locate and retrieve a strange, alien broadcasting device in the Arctic. A device Crowley instinctively knew had been sent by some eldritch race, and which apparently had the ability to raise the dead.

Yet again, the airship *Dacdalus* and her crew interceded, killing Hummel and stealing the artifact. Crowley had been inconsolable with the loss...until his agents intercepted

AEGIS transmissions regarding a reopening of the dimensional rift on Noble's Isle.

Maria had returned.

His lost protege survived more than a year in a strange dimension, among those same arthropoid demons, returning with new arcane knowledge. She was changed. Stronger, somehow. More radiant with power. While Crowley still had superior knowledge in terms of scholastics and reference, Maria was now in possession of far greater sheer will than even the self-described Great Beast of Mankind.

The past six months had been a time for reconnection. For reflection. And a renewal of plans for the destruction of their enemies at AEGIS. More personnel were recruited. More weapons of war and chaos deployed. Their plans were now on a scale unheard of before Maria's reappearance, vast and complex. They could afford to be.

"Maria," Crowley muttered over a sip of wine. He returned his gaze to the flickering fire.

The woman shifted with a barely concealed excitement. "Yes, my Master," she replied in an accent tinged with German. She used the honorific out of habit, and it worked to conceal her rising aspirations.

"I have an operation underway in North America. I want you to take command."

Maria smiled and took another sip of claret. "With pleasure, my Master."

"This will be an endeavor far larger than any of our previous rituals. We are summoning the Elder Gods, the great Old Ones that exist in the outer voids of space. You will need to be a conduit for my efforts. Amplifying my power."

"Understood, my Master." Maria felt his new ambition wash over her like the wave of an opium high. So, they were opening a portal to welcome in as many of the Old Ones as cared to come through, to wreak chaos and destruction upon the pitiful mortals of the world. A step up from a single demon, or even the many arachnids they'd summoned in the past. And yet, eminently possible.

Crowley let his upper lip curl into a subtle smile. "Good. Because it does mean the annihilation of the *Daedalus* and her crew."

Maria raised her goblet in a toast. "So much the better, my Master."

- CHAPTER 1 -

Peru, June 1929

The French airliner roared into the moonlight over Rio Huaruro, banking hard against the headwind clobbering it from the canyon ahead. A battered Bréguet 26T with an expired registry, the biplane jostled and bounced with each new air current, almost approximating a rafting experience on the whitewater rapids below. The aircraft struggled to maintain altitude between ridges of snowy peaks to either side, and inconsistent winds rushing up from the riverbed. She was flown by a local hire and carried two men and a woman as fares, each clad in dusty gray fatigues and wilderness gear.

"We should not have left Hans," said one, his accent tinged with an Austrian lilt.

"Then he shouldn't have allowed himself to become distracted," said the other, his voice a baritone English growl.

The woman spoke in a crisp American accent, clutching a leather satchel in front of her, feeling its weight. "Hans has become one with the Master." She glanced between the two men, each a rugged soldier. "And if we do not get the *camasca* stone to him without delay, we can expect the same." She scowled, noting internally that the two men were good field agents and more than useful as tomb robbers, but the bickering on this mission had been a nearly constant source of stress. "I'm going up to speak to the pilot," she announced, ducking her head under the satchel's leather strap and taking its contents with her.

Like many early airliners, the Bréguet had a passenger compartment enclosed within the main fuselage, with a single or two-pilot cockpit above and forward. The helm of the 26T had the advantage of being enclosed from the elements, when many of her contemporaries would have been open to the air and inaccessible from the main cabin.

Stepping up a short ladder and nosing through the musty drapes separating the two spaces, the woman could see the Peruvian pilot grapple with the flight control stick. The plane jostled with a powerful gust from the canyon, and the woman braced herself on the wooden steps to keep from falling back into the passenger compartment.

"How long to the airstrip at Andamayo?" she asked, grunting against the jostling of the aircraft.

The pilot startled at the question, bristling somewhat. "There is no airstrip in Andamayo, *señora*."

"There must be a mistake." The woman ran a slender finger across her brow, corralling a stray lock of blond hair to hang behind her right ear. "The deal was to get us to Andamayo."

The pilot shook his head under the brim of a worn bush hat. "I'm sorry, *señora*. I cannot land the plane where there is no place to land. It is roughly eighty miles to Camaná. Your contacts await you at the harbor."

"Why is the air so turbulent?"

"Because, *señora*, my plane can barely fly above the mountains unloaded, let alone with passengers. So I must fly the canyon. And flying the canyon will keep us hidden from outside view."

The woman nodded in understanding. "Very well. Carry on, *señor*," she said, retreating through the drapery and down the ladder to the passenger compartment.

"We are eighty miles to Camaná," she informed her fellow agents. "It will be a bumpy ride, but at least we'll be hard to follow. Even if the AEGIS agents did manage to track our takeoff."

A thousand feet above and behind the passenger plane, a second aircraft dropped out of the night sky. It was a Vought O2U Corsair, painted black with a chrome engine cowling and pirate markings on the wings and fuselage. Its Pratt & Whitney radial engine bellowed like a nightmarish beast, two elegant sets of wings silhouetted against a pale moon.

The man in the rear cockpit was a broad-shouldered figure, dark eyes peering through a pair of flight goggles under a leather helmet. Pinching the radio's *TALK* mechanism at his throat, he growled in a basso West Indies accent, "There they are!"

In the forward cockpit, another tall figure nodded, flashing a thumbs-up to the pilot behind him. "Affirmative," he radioed back. "See if you can come up right above their aft left quarter."

There was a short pause, then the pilot hailed again. "You're going to board them?"

"I thought I would, yes."

"You know I have three guns on this bird. We could shoot them down."

"And risk losing or damaging the *camasca* stone? No thanks, Stede."

"Jack, you realize the chief property of the artifact is in the name—it's made of stone."

"We made a promise to the chief."

"Fair enough," the pilot chuckled deep within his chest. "Get ready, Captain Stratosphere."

Jack McGraw pushed himself up in the forward seat, flinging his right leg over the outside of the fuselage, a black leather officer's boot kicking against the painted flag which displayed the arms of the historical gentleman pirate Stede Bonnet. A white skull grinned above a horizontal long bone, centered between a dagger and a heart.

The biplane's pilot—and the namesake of Bonnet—barked into the radio set once again. "Ay, watch it! This is a fresh paint job!"

Jack paused, glaring back at the other pilot momentarily before shaking his head and sliding a spring clip through a utility bracket on the outer fuselage, just forward of the rear pilot compartment. The clip attached to a thin metal cable, which in turn connected to a harness Jack wore over his gray leather AEGIS flight jacket. He stepped carefully to the inside right wing, clutching the N-shaped aluminum brace with gloved hands. They were coming up behind the passenger plane fast.

Jack squatted next to the wing brace and did some quick flight geometry in his head, estimating angle and distance. Gesturing with his right hand like a plane wing, he instructed Stede to bank and cross the aft quarter of the Bréguet. Then he snaked the same hand through a leather strap attached to the rear grip of a nickel-plated 45 Colt automatic, shucking the pistol from its chest holster. The lanyard tugged at his wrist in the wind as he wrapped the same arm around the wing brace. Winding a couple of loops of aluminum cable around his right hand, he set his jaw and took a deep breath.

Inside the larger plane, the Austrian man caught motion outside the left side passenger windows and went to investigate more closely. Brushing aside the cabin curtains, he had just enough time to see the Corsair bank away to the left, then angle over right, across their tail.

"*Scheisse!*" he exclaimed, drawing the attention of his two partners, just before a series of gunshots blazed through the exterior cabin door.

The British agent cried out and staggered to the left side of the cabin, stomach perforated with Colt slugs.

As the Austrian and the American woman each drew a sidearm, the cabin door collapsed inward with a deafening crunch, sending splinters of wood and fabric spinning into the passenger compartment. Suddenly Jack was crouched in front of them, his muscular form filling up the rear of the plane as the canyon wind whistled by the open hatch.

The blond woman gasped. "It's him. It's McGraw."

The Austrian raised a Mauser pistol and took aim, but before he could fire, the plane was hit by a mammoth gust of wind from the canyon. It suddenly nosed up, sending the agent careening toward Jack.

Catching the man in a boxing hug, Jack held tightly as the plane dropped once again, and the cable pulled both men back out through the door. Jack felt his stomach plunge as he spun away into the open canyon, suspended only by the thin cable to Stede's Corsair above. He let go his grip on the Austrian agent and kicked, sending the man wind-milling into the chasm below. A thin trail of acrid gray smoke began to waft behind the agent before he impacted on the river rocks a thousand feet down.

Stede banked the Corsair again, and Jack found himself swinging back toward the ene-my plane. He'd been lucky with his entry the first time. The second time would not be a sure thing. As he approached, the Latécoère suddenly dropped, and Jack braced as his left leg impacted the top right of the plane, rolling across the body and off the right side. He hoped Stede didn't over-correct, which had the potential to send him flailing into the north canyon wall. Fortunately his old friend was an experienced pilot, and Jack came nowhere close to the rocks. His stomach lurched as he made contact with the top of the plane a third time, coming down squarely on all fours.

Stede watched his friend slide about-face, planting a boot under the upper wing assem-bly. The sky pirate dropped the Corsair down slightly to give the cable a few feet of slack. Seizing the opportunity, Jack grabbed hold of the open hatchway and pulled himself down, flipping into the plane a second time, releasing the cable from his harness. If he was knocked out of the door again, there would be no re-turn—and no parachute to slow his fall.

The Brit crouched with his own pistol at the ready, already consumed with tendrils of black smoke that smelled of incense, brimstone, and burning flesh. A shot rang out, causing Jack to flinch in response. The British agent collapsed to the floor, crumbling to a smoldering pile of dust and fragments of bone.

Jack turned his head sharply to see the blond woman backed against the bulkhead near the stepladder to the cockpit. Smoke wafted from the barrel of her sidearm, and Jack noticed a peculiar—and familiar—pain in his right shoulder, at the junction of the pectoral muscle. He could feel his own pistol dangling from the lanyard around his right wrist, and every inch of real estate between those two points throbbed in agony. Fortunately, it was a clean shot, as evidenced by the hole in the rear wall behind him. He screwed up every ounce of courage he could, making himself large and imposing within the passenger compartment, an easy task given his height and the low ceiling.

"Give up the *camasca* stone," he ordered. "Nobody else needs to get hurt."

The woman threw Jack a wistful smile. "Sorry, Captain. If I am to be free of the Soul Bond with the Master, I must lay this at his feet."

"Sounds like a choice you made," Jack sighed. It was a retort handed down from his father, who always kept it handy for those times when young Jack McGraw found himself in dire straits. It was a surgical nod to personal responsibility, but sometimes it could be just a bit insensitive.

As he flipped the dangling Colt back into his right hand, the plane bucked again, rising on a cushion of canyon air.

The blond agent fell forward toward the rear of the cabin, firing into Jack's center of mass, but the Mauser jammed. Jack fired his Colt at the same time, but the slider clicked back, and Jack knew his pistol was empty. Then the woman made impact, knocking the breath from his lungs and causing his shoulder to scream in absolute agony. Grunting and cursing, the two rolled and tumbled to the back of the plane.

They hit the rear bulkhead with Jack's wounded shoulder first, and as the agent pushed away to open some distance and perhaps clear her pistol, she stumbled backward, and suddenly found herself hanging out of the open cabin door. Her left hand grasped his harness, while his left found itself tangled in the strap from the satchel.

Realizing the position she was now in, the woman kicked against the fuselage, trying to pull Jack out of the open door with her.

Cringing, Jack braced his wounded arm inside the cabin and tried to haul her back inside.

Perhaps knowing he wasn't about to let the satchel go, she released his harness with her left hand and began working the slider on the Mauser pistol to clear the jam. Wind whistled through her loose hair as her legs pedaled over the empty canyon below them.

The plane rolled left, and Jack's arm flared with burning strain as he desperately clutched the satchel and the enemy agent attached to it. He glanced up at the Corsair and saw Stede give him a two-fingered visor salute.

"Aww, come on!" Jack grunted almost silently into the wind.

As if in response, Stede banked the Corsair to the right, and the other pilot panicked, rolling the passenger biplane in kind.

Bracing his booted left foot against the agent's torso as her weight returned to him, Jack shoved with all of his strength, watching sadly as her arm slipped out of the shoulder strap.

She dropped like a brick into the canyon valley, trailing black smoke as she fell.

Jack blinked, realizing he'd kicked hard enough to propel himself to the cabin floor, the heavy satchel now resting atop his chest. He scrambled upright, taking a quick peek inside the bag. There was the *camasca* stone, looted from the tomb of a revered and powerful *yatiri*, or healer, of the Aymara people. A beautiful length of translucent green quartz roughly the size of a police billy club, the stone was intricately carved with incantations of protection and healing. Not that it would have been used for such benign purpose by its erstwhile captors. Fortunately, it was now one less artifact to power the sinister magic of Aleister Crowley. One less win for the *Astrum Argentum*.

Now, he thought. *How best to get off this plane...*

He could signal Stede to lower the cable back down, secure it to the harness and make his escape that way, but with his shoulder wound he could not be sure of climbing back up to the Corsair. So that was no good.

He could get Stede to bring his plane under the Bréguet, and he could lower down to the Corsair, but again, his shoulder was the wildcard. No, he would have to see about taking over the passenger plane

Jack staggered completely to his feet, pushing his flight goggles to his forehead. He grabbed hold of the Colt from its lanyard, popping out the magazine and producing a replacement from his belt. Slapping it into the grip and loading a round into the chamber with a pull of the slide, he moved forward through the cabin, inching toward the cockpit. Pulling the drapes aside, he led with the pistol in his right hand.

Another gunshot greeted him, this time clipping his left shoulder, leaving a torn shred of bloodied cowhide in its wake. Jack spun to the side of the portal. "You gotta be kidding me!" he muttered, glancing down at his grazed shoulder in disbelief. With his still-throbbing right hand, he raised the Colt and fired three barking shots at an upward angle, figuring that with the pilot at a raised station, he was more likely to score a hit without damaging controls or instruments.

The plane suddenly dropped, and Jack knew he'd hit his target.

Eyes wide with adrenaline, he scampered quickly to the pilot compartment and saw the man slumped over in his chair. Hauling the dead pilot backwards, out of the seat and down into the main cabin, he stole a glance at the instrument panel. The plane was steadily losing altitude as the stick drifted lazily back and forth. On either side, the mountains loomed. Before him, the canyon walls converged to a narrow chasm.

Immediately, Jack clambered into the chair and tested the stick. It felt like moving a paddle through molasses. He wasn't used to a beast like the Bréguet, but at least now she was relatively empty. Throttling forward to pick up as much speed as possible, he rolled the stick hard left, and felt the wings tilt as the bulky passenger plane heeled over sideways and high stone walls closed in on him.

- CHAPTER 2 -

"Damn that brick-headed daredevil!"

Stede cursed under his breath and pulled up over the tight canyon mouth, making use of the Corsair's service ceiling and a welcome updraft. Following the craggy line of the chasm below, he watched for any sign of fire, smoke, impact, or explosion. If Captain Stratosphere was to perish in this valley tonight, Stede would have to bring his body—whatever there was left of it—back to Doc, or she would raise holy hell. And he knew that wasn't just a metaphor.

The Corsair raced ahead at full throttle, finally reaching the canyon exit. Stede pulled the biplane around in a wide, banking turn, wings silhouetted in the Peruvian night sky. The river tumbled from the mouth of the chasm, rushing and racing onto the rocks of the canyon floor. There was no sign of the Bréguet.

A horrible reality started to sink in, and Stede began to look for a plateau where he could put down and track the top of the chasm on foot.

The Bréguet suddenly shot from the mouth of the canyon, leveling out as it lost altitude. The outboard landing gear dipped into the churning whitewater and the plane climbed sharply, banking into a hard left turn as the Colca Canyon intersected with another craggy alpine finger from the northwest. The river surged against the ancient stone as it made a hairpin cut to the south.

Stede tracked the larger aircraft from above, wondering what Jack would do. It was still roughly an hour's flight time to Camaná on the Pacific coast. Although his Corsair was in good shape to make the voyage, there was a lot of rough canyon between their current position and a more hospitable landing area, and he wasn't sure how the Bréguet was set for fuel. His silent question was answered as the passenger biplane suddenly banked across the

canyon lip and headed west toward Andamayo. The Corsair followed.

The local pilot had been correct in that
there was not an airstrip in the small mountain village, but there was an open field, pur-
posely left fallow for crop rotation. Populated
by the indigenous Aymara, this tiny, level valley was lush with summer crops, watered by
direct irrigation from the Rio Colca. Housing
ran the gamut from thatched huts to clapboard shanties, and a pitted dirt road ran
through the village, hugging the western edge
of the canyon as it continued south to the
coast.

At the rear of the open field sat a small dirigible, tied down to special pitons driven into
the earth at angles. It was lozenge-shaped,
with a mirror-finish aluminum envelope. A tail
assembly of stabilizers sprouted from the rear,
and a large thrust engine rested at the end of
an outboard strut on each side. Just under
250 feet long, and about half that in width, it
was a sleek bullet, with a narrow gondola running fore and aft, and a small bridge protrud-
ing from the underside of the nose.

Her registry read *LR3-01*, the name displayed on the side: *Daedalus*.

Though there were no landing lights on the
field, the soft, even moonlight created a basic

outline to work from. Additionally, the airship had both front spotlights illuminated, casting a pallid glow across an area that would be growing maize the following year.

The passenger plane came in low and bounced to a short landing, flaps raised to brake. It taxied to the far end of the field and waited for Stede and the Corsair to come in. The pirate plane followed in the path of the Bréguet, pulling to a halt in half the distance. Engines sputtered and cranked down, propellers lurching to a stop.

A crowd of locals emerged from the gray darkness.

The woman standing among the gathered Aymara was in her mid-thirties, tall and athletic, a naturally-wavy chestnut bob framing a pleasing, heart-shaped face. She wore an AEGIS Aeronautics field uniform, and discerning green eyes scanned the shadows for the plane's occupants.

Her Cherokee crewmate stood to her right, wearing a matching uniform and casually clutching a Winchester repeating carbine. Dark brown eyes peered from a sunbaked face into the sundered passenger hatch for any sign of movement within. Jet-black, close-cropped hair ruffled in the canyon breeze.

Suddenly Jack McGraw's large frame filled the doorway, followed by his equally-broad smile.

Though not officially married by law, Dorothy "Doc" Starr and Captain McGraw had a daughter together and lived for all intents and purposes as a family. They were also quite the power couple within AEGIS, their exploits well-known both within the organization and without, thanks to a popular movie serial produced by Universal Studios.

She strode to him as he stepped down, flattening him against the fuselage with a passionate kiss, and immediately regretting it when his entire body tensed.

"Ow! Shoulder!"

Doc winced in sympathy, biting her lower lip. "Ooh. Sorry. I'll take a look when we...say, did you get the stone?"

Jack managed to find her eyes in the falloff from the airship lights, winking at her. "It's in the bag, sweetheart."

Doc looked confused. "So what else do you need to—"

"No, really," Jack interrupted. "The stone is *actually* in the bag." He carefully shrugged out of the satchel's strap and handed the heavy parcel to Doc.

The local Aymara tentatively drew closer, encircling the couple. An ancient man in a straw hat and homespun poncho approached from the crowd as Doc draw the *camasca* stone from the canvas bag. The emerald quartz caught the light from the *Daedalus* and seemed to channel it into its own remarkable version, casting out a blanket of rippling caustics, almost like illumination from a pool of water.

"Muy bien," the old man muttered in a voice like a campfire. "You save the *camasca*."

Jack gave the *yatiri* a solemn nod. "It's back where it belongs now."

Doc, still somewhat transfixed by the hypnotic light refraction through the stone, blinked and shook the cobwebs away. "Yes," she agreed, handing it to the old man. "And if anyone tries to take it from you again, don't hesitate to call."

A genuine, gap-toothed smile broke across the shaman's grizzled face, eyes twinkling in the glow from the stone as he accepted it. "We make a stronger magic," he assured Doc. "Make more safe." Punctuating the sentiment, two younger Aymara stepped forward, each holding a repeating rifle at the ready. The *yatiri* gestured at the younger men. *"Guardianes. Protectores."*

"We've got a new headquarters in Caracas as well, so if you need anything..." Stede Bonnet stepped from the crowd to join Jack and Doc in the middle of the circle. A small monkey had appeared from the mass of people and was now riding the sky pirate's left shoulder like an Indian elephant driver. Stede reached up and gave Jake-in-Irons a scratch behind the ear as the monkey chirped and squealed in delight.

"*Gracias.*" nodded the old man, delicately hefting the stone in his withered hands. "*Tu la cábala.*"

Jack squinted, the pain in his shoulder really starting to throb. "*No entiendo.*"

"*Cábala.*" Stede repeated, leaning in close. "Like a secret family."

The old man nodded emphatically. "*Si! Familia secreta!*"

Several people in the crowd, mostly grandmothers with kindly, weather-worn faces, pressed in, imploring the adventurers from the sky to stay and rest in their village. Blankets of woven alpaca wool were thrust into the arms of Jack, Doc, and Stede. One old woman reached up and laid a necklace of handmade beads around the Cherokee's neck.

Jack winced under the sudden load of gifts. "I think that's our cue."

"Agreed," Doc muttered, muffled by another folded blanket on a growing stack. "Deadeye, tell Cipher we're leaving."

"Affirmative," the sharpshooter replied, clearing the folding gondola steps with a single leap.

"Good flying with you again, Captain," Stede nudged Jack in his bloody shoulder, causing a flood of stabbing pain from the wound.

Jack grunted. "You too, Stede. You staying?"

"Not much choice. Gotta wait for one of my guys to come retrieve my salvaged Bréguet."

"Your salvaged...?" Jack feigned shock. "I guess it's the least we could do."

"The very least," Stede laughed. "What about the renegade pilot?" He nodded toward the airliner's cockpit.

"Dead," Jack muttered softly. "We know he's wanted by the authorities for smuggling and other criminal transport. You can keep the bounty."

Stede looked pleased. "This day has become quite lucrative for me! And all I had to do was dump you out of my plane."

Jack shook his head with a weary smile. "If I ever need to get dumped out of a plane in the future—"

"Any time, my friend," Stede saluted as the locals pushed closer.

Doc wanted to wave, but both hands were pinned under a load of native crafts. She sufficed with a nod as she and Jack extricated themselves from the swelling crowd. "Don't be a stranger."

"Stranger than what?" Stede grinned, winking at her as they climbed aboard the *Daedalus.*

Jack took a last look from the gondola door. "Stranger than usual," he chuckled. "Good flying, Captain Bonnet!"

"Good flying, Captain Stratosphere!"

Deadeye hauled up the steps, and they were away. The giant outboard engines spun into action, whirring from a low drone to a high-pitched, warm buzz like a hive of bees. The slightly-flattened football-shaped envelope of the *Daedalus* light recon airship lifted into the night sky over the Colca Canyon, nosing northward. Within minutes, her running lights had merged with a field of stars strewn across the colorful band of the Milky Way, lost in the Peruvian night sky.

- CHAPTER 3 -

At cruising speed, the 3,800-mile distance back to West Orange, New Jersey would take just over 34 hours, provided the weather held and no serious headwinds were encountered.

The engine room lay aft of the main crew compartment, and just forward of the small cargo bay. It housed ten proprietary electric dynamos which powered all systems on the light airship, and currently accommodated the ship's engineer. Dhakiya "Sparks" Kitur, Kenyan airplane mechanic and erstwhile Kikuyu princess, sat at her primary control panel, booted feet resting atop the counter surface as she leaned back in a perforated metal chair. She was dressed in similar fashion to her crewmates, at least from the waist down: officer's boots; navy trousers; and a pale gray cotton work shirt, sleeves rolled to the elbows. She wore a dark mechanic's vest instead of the leather flight jacket, and flipped through a saddle-stitched technical manual which was, for all intents and purposes, an interpretation of her field upgrade to the DiMarco-Edison generators.

Sparks was impressed. If she'd been reading about any other engineering advancement, she'd assume its architect was a genius. Not bad for an orphan from a rural village under British occupation.

On the bridge, Deadeye sat at the port-side radio console, listening into a pair of headphones, his chin resting in the palm of his hand while he caught a quick cat nap. Leaning over the desk wasn't quite as comfortable as lounging in the top turret harness, but Charlie Dalton could doze just about anywhere, under any conditions.

Marissa Singh occupied the pilot's seat, smartly dressed in the AEGIS Aeronautics Division field uniform. Her raven hair was braided and pinned under a red service beret with the AEGIS winged shield and sword insignia on the patch, crimson bindi displayed below the band. Singh, known among the crew by the call sign "Cipher", ordinarily sat at comms, her ability to translate complex codes in a dozen languages legendary within the AEGIS operation. She was also a qualified LR3 skipper, which gave her a secondary role as relief pilot—and a much-needed break from the radio—when Captain McGraw was getting stitched up.

And that happened more often than one might think.

After the crew's Arctic adventure of the previous autumn, the unoccupied sixth crew quarters had been commandeered as a rudimentary sick bay. Jack McGraw now sat on the edge of the aluminum bunk, shirtless to the waist, toned frame displaying clusters of bruises in brown and purple, crosshatched in red abrasions. The expanse of his back, shoulders, and ribs looked like a topographical map, with scars from bullets and blades forming various mountain ranges and lakes. Just 34, McGraw had a physical age closer to 50. He had more miles on him, figuratively and literally, than the vast majority of his peers.

He was 20 when he started flying for the RFC on the Western Front, which some would have reckoned enough action for one lifetime. But after the war, he and Deadeye kicked around Europe, fighting fascists in Italy and generally raising hell for a couple of years. Back in the States, the life of a test pilot and aeronautics consultant was positively idyllic by comparison.

But then Dorothy walked back into his life, and the past four years had been one crazy adventure after another.

Doc sat next to the bunk in a lightweight aluminum chair, tending his injuries, much as she'd done over the past four years, and during the war. Her patient shifted the ice compress from his bruised collar bone, and she nodded at it, admonishing him to keep the pack in place. She finished sewing his shoulder wound, clipping the silk thread with a long-handled pair of surgical scissors. Though focused on her medical task, her bow lips pursed into a thoughtful *O*.

"I would've liked to have some time examining the *camasca* stone, you know."

Jack winced as the scissor blades tugged at the suture. "Yeah, I know," he admitted. "But this wasn't some ancient artifact of a dead culture, or even a gift from a living one."

She knew he referred to the Dagger of Lir, a Celtic ceremonial object they'd procured from a thousand-year-old tomb on the Scottish island of Scarba, and the Athena Vambrace, a bronze armor piece given to Doc by their field contact in Greece. She also had to concede he had a point.

"The Aymara culture is still very much alive," Jack continued, "and that *camasca* stone has spiritual importance to them. It's all well and good as long as it doesn't fall into Silver Star hands...again."

It was true. Most of the artifacts of mystical power they'd "rescued" or "liberated" were not going to be missed by a present culture, nor were they placed into a museum for public display. They were going to a hidden laboratory to be studied and cataloged away under lock and key, safe from misuse by the *Astrum Argentum*. But the Aymara people of the Andes were alive and vital, at least as much as any other indigenous culture in the post-colonial Western hemisphere.

"Sounds like the Aymara have seen to that possibility," Doc offered, applying a bandage over the suture site.

Jack inhaled sharply through his teeth.

"Procaine not working?" Doc asked.

A subdued chuckle escaped Jack's lips. "Must be developing a tolerance," he quipped. "You know, what with all the daring heroics..."

"Speaking of which," Doc interjected, raising an eyebrow, "as your physician, I recommend you reduce your bullet intake." She rolled the squeaky rubber gloves from her hands, placing them in the open medical bag next to her.

Jack held up a finger in sarcastic protest. "But...the heroics..."

Doc closed up the bag and shook her head of chestnut curls. "No heroics," she affirmed.

"What about unflinching courage?"

"Absolutely no unflinching courage."

"How about some derring-do? Can we at least have derring-do?"

Doc made a face of comical shock. "Derring-do?! Why, Captain, the very idea! What kind of girl do you think I am?"

"The kind who has derring-do with a strange man out of wedlock."

Doc smiled so radiantly Jack could feel the temperature in the room spike by a few degrees. "That's true," she winked, leaving a casual nibble on his lower lip. "You are a strange man."

"You have no idea," Jack said, almost a whisper, leaning in slowly. Doc reached up to cradle his face in her hands, and their lips merged in a passionate kiss.

"Oh yes I do," she said, sliding from the chair onto his lap. "I'm your physician."

They continued trading kisses, and Jack managed a bemused, "I've never had a doctor take such a personal interest."

Doc laughed softly, easing his head back onto the bunk and sliding down with him.

"You're a very special patient, Captain Mc-Graw..."

- CHAPTER 4 -

The *Daedalus* arrived over southwestern New Jersey just after 6:30 p.m. local time, speeding over fields and tiny rural townships as the sun dipped below the horizon. By the time they reached their destination, it was dusk, and the lights began to flicker on below.

If Kenilworth Airfield had been a busy hub of AEGIS activity the previous year, its traffic looked to be at least twice that of before. The six-hangar plane facility had doubled capacity, and the two massive aerodromes were glowing with work lights and 24-hour technical crews seeing to the work of the Aeronautics division. The control tower had been enlarged, and the small neighborhood of pilot and worker bungalows seemed three times its initial size, sprawling to the southwest of the open field.

Not content to have the main Aeronautics facility hooked up to the ever-expanding municipal grid, AEGIS co-founder Thomas Edison had seen to it that Kenilworth had its own independent power station, running dozens of scaled-up versions of the same dynamo generators that powered the *Daedalus*. The station itself was deep underground as a defense against aerial attack, marked only by a nondescript cinder block building near the control tower.

An open electric tram ran along a charged track around the outside of the airfield in an oblong circuit, taking workers to and from the aerodromes, the commissary, the residences, and points in between.

Jack scanned out the bridge windscreen array and whistled through his teeth. From the sky, it looked like a bustling industrial city of the future.

"Clearance to land on Baker pad," Cipher announced, back at the Comms station. "West end, near the north aerodrome." She added, "Thank you, Tower," and turned to Jack with a grin. "Tower says, 'Welcome home, Captain Stratosphere.'"

Jack winced, eyes rolling back in their sockets. He would truly never be rid of his nickname from the Great War.

Doc cackled from the Navigation station opposite Comms. She rarely tired of reminding him of it herself. The torment was even more delicious when others did it for her.

Jack nosed the *Daedalus* toward the designated landing area and a small ground crew came out to meet them. In moments, the airship was cleated down, outboard thruster blades spinning down to a halt.

Jack, Doc, and Cipher exited the starboard-side gondola door, fold-down steps deployed by one of the ground crew. Sparks and Deadeye exited aft, via the cargo bay ramp, which wheezed down on hydraulic pistons.

A slender woman in the cotton summer AEGIS uniform of royal blue, displaying the patches and insignia for the Security division, approached from the control tower. She wore the same navy blue trousers and black officer's boots as the crew, dark hair pulled back in a braided bun under a garrison cap, finger waves framing a round face. She passed under the broad white beam of an airfield floodlight, and Doc's face lit up to match.

"Sarah!" she exclaimed, stepping in to meet the woman in a friendly hug.

Jack grinned out of half of his face. "Agent Chin!" he boomed. "I figured AEGIS was up to no good when they reassigned you from the ranch."

The woman reached out, pulling Jack into an embrace. "So good to see you, Captain, Doc..." Thumbing the rank pip on her collar, she added, "and it's Lieutenant Chin now."

"Yep, up to no good!" Jack laughed.

Sarah Chin was the daughter of a war hero, Henry Chin, one of a handful of Chinese-Americans to serve in the Great War, a member of the Lost Battalion slaughtered in the Argonne Forest. She'd joined AEGIS right out of high school, initially content to serve on a security force assigned to Jack and Doc's ranch in her native Los Angeles. But clearly someone in Admin was grooming her for bigger things.

"Welcome back," she said formally. "I'm to escort you to the medical center at Glenmont to get you all checked out."

Deadeye and Sparks joined the congregation from behind.

"Checked out?" Deadeye mused, louder than anticipated. Sarah heard him.

"You've been on assignment in the tropics," she explained. "It's standard procedure now."

Doc laughed. "I'm all for letting someone else check over this crew."

Lieutenant Chin cocked her head toward the flight control tower and the parking area beyond. "Come on," she said. "I have a car waiting."

The automobile she referred to was a brand-new Packard limousine, red and black with suicide doors and a uniformed chauffeur. The crew piled in the rear seating area, noting what a change the crushed velvet interior was in contrast to the airship they spent most of their time in. Sarah Chin slid into the front passenger seat.

The trip to the Glenmont compound was short and uneventful, and the guard at the gate waved them through without delay. Jack and Doc were both surprised, however, when the car failed to turn toward the front parking circle of the brick mansion, instead continuing deeper onto the property. It passed the research laboratory and primary workshop, finally pulling to a stop in front of the massive barn which had originally housed the second *Daedalus* prototype. It had been whitewashed since their last visit, a large red cross painted on the giant sliding door. Apparently, the old hangar was now a medical center.

Jack paused as his crew stepped from the limo, everyone taking in the change. Jack and Doc recalled arriving here in the pink light of dawn, April 1925, as the ground crew first led the *Daedalus II* from the cavernous wooden structure. They remembered how the airship's vulcanized canvas envelope shimmered in the morning light, helium ballonets tugging at the mooring cables.

"Remember seeing the old bird in the daylight?" Jack sighed.

Doc leaned her head against his shoulder. "Seems like forever ago."

Sarah checked them in at the main entrance, a smaller, human-sized door to the side of the massive slider. They were escorted into a labyrinth of office walls, exam rooms, and test facilities. While Chin waited in the front reception area, a dour-looking matron directed each crewmember to a separate examination room, where they were subjected to a routine physical, including a blood draw.

A middle-aged doctor of African extraction, with reading specs and a mustache dusted with silver, checked the wound dressing on Jack's shoulder and pronounced Doc's needlework exemplary. Jack laughed and said he'd pass the word, not that it would be a surprise to her. She'd learned her trade sewing bloody wounds at the Western Front, waist-deep in unspeakable muck, mud, and viscera. A quick listen to breathing and heartbeat, a check of reflexes, and another quip about avoiding bullets, and the doctor proclaimed Jack relatively healthy, all things considered.

He returned to the lobby, finding he was the last to be cleared. The rest of the crew stood in a small circle of conversation with Sarah and an Asian man in a dapper brown three-piece suit. Private detective David Li was visiting Glenmont from New York City, where AEGIS had stumbled on a breakthrough. The Silver Star were apparently backing a Chinatown tong whose major industry happened to be trafficking a mind-control drug distilled from Martian "Red Weed". Used in conjunction with opium to help reduce resistance, this drug had now spread to the community at large, and had been a factor in several murders. But Li and his undercover partner had recently located the manufacturing facility upstate. They were assembling a strike team at Glenmont to shut down the drug lab, and Li was waiting on what he called his "big gun" to get cleared by the Medical Division.

When Jack heard this big gun was former heavyweight champion John Mabry, he was shocked. "I heard Mabry died in Egypt a couple years ago," he frowned.

David Li raised an eyebrow in his direction and added, "He did."

They took their leave of the private eye and walked as a group across the property to the main house. Jack shook his head in disbelief.

"So we're using undead prizefighters now?"

Sarah Chin laughed aloud. "How long has it been since you checked in with Shaw?" She referred to Colonel Stephen Shaw, AEGIS London Bureau Chief.

"About two years ago?" Doc squinted, recalling their trip to the underground facility in Scotland, where the wreckage of Martian tripod walkers from the invasion of 1894 was revealed to them.

Cipher wrinkled her nose. "Consider that since then, we secured an alien beacon that raises the dead."

"Oh, well we've been dealing with dead things ever since we started this little club," Deadeye drawled, only half-joking. "Voodoo zombies, rocket-ghouls, reanimated mummies, not to mention those spider demons from the island..." A chill ran down his spine and he visibly shuddered.

"And *Bwana Kifo*," Sparks added, remembering the enormous, skull-painted African warrior known for escaping—or rather, repelling—physical death, and how he'd come to the aid of the Kikuyu when British troops were set on the local villages in her native Kenya.

Chin nodded. "When your enemy is the Silver Star, fighting demons and the undead is part of the deal. And sometimes that means fighting fire with fire." As they angled onto a gravel path that led back to the manor, she continued. "Shaw has put together a field team consisting of a Gurkha shock trooper, a robot with a human brain, a vampire, a gunfighting ghost, and a powerful blind psychic."

"Sounds like the beginning of a joke about a barkeep," Jack quipped.

"Just a second," Doc blinked, halting in her tracks. "Blind psychic? I wonder if it's Joe Desmond."

Sarah Chin cast a look of shocked surprise at Doc. "That's exactly who it is."

"Someone you know?" Jack asked.

Doc recalled the memory through a look of bemusement. "Toward the end of the war. He was with the 369th New York—the Harlem Hellfighters. Came through my hospital. He'd been exposed to a combination of chemical weapons at the battle to take Ripont and left for dead. Revived spontaneously. The gas had blinded him, but also unleashed some powerful extrasensory abilities."

"Sounds like a good guy to have on our side," Jack muttered. "Mabry, too."

They arrived at the rear entry to the palatial home, and Sarah held the door open, waving them into yet another reception area. "Come on," she said. "Mr. Edison wanted to see you as soon as your exams were finished."

The *Daedalus* crew filed through the entry, as a smaller Packard rolled past toward the driveway checkpoint. Two lab technicians sat in the backseat, a leather valise between them. A guard searched the car trunk and then pawed through the valise, finding nothing of interest. They were waved through, and the car turned east toward the Hudson River, and Manhattan. When they were out of sight of Edison's compound, the techs exchanged a knowing glance. One pulled a small glass vial with a rubber stopper from his inside breast pocket, holding the blood sample up to the streetlight glare. He nodded, smiling devilishly at the other.

The Master would have his spell components after all.

- CHAPTER 5 -

They found Thomas Edison in the second-floor living room, behind an enormous executive desk of oak and walnut. A balding pate and fringe of white hair was visible over a mountain of file folders, reference tomes, and various notebooks and ledgers. A phonograph console bearing his name and likeness blasted the strains of the MacDowell Sisters' 1924 recording of *Baby Sister Blues*, a crooning vocal duet with ukulele and lap steel. Now 82 and almost completely deaf, Edison had been crazy for Hawaiian music for years, and the MacDowell Sisters from Dallas, Texas, were one of his favorite acts.

Sarah approached the desk and waved over the stack of papers to get his attention.

"Sir? I have the *Daedalus* crew to see you, as ordered."

Edison's concentration shifted toward the interruption, and he stood with a grunt to switch off the phonograph. When he turned to face the visitors, his face lit up in recognition.

"Aha! My friends! Come in!" he greeted, ambling toward the group with an uncertain gait but his right hand extended. "Jack, my boy! Dorothy! Good to see you! All of you! You are all quite welcome!"

Doc's smile was laced with pity. The Wizard of Menlo Park now walked with a pronounced shuffle, his body angled forward. Although the gossip columns claimed he was in the thrall of the fad diet *du jour*, Doc knew that he didn't ascribe to those movements, and ate from a mostly healthy vegetarian menu. His sallow complexion and the bags under his eyes were due more to lack of sleep than to poor nutrition. She also worried about a potential underlying kidney ailment, but she was not his physician, and would not presume to insert herself into that relationship.

Jack shook the old inventor's gnarled hand, and Doc leaned in to land a peck on his cheek, which gave him a bashful glow.

Edison worked his way through the group, shaking every hand without exception. "How are you? How do you do? Welcome back! How was...Brazil, was it?"

"Peru, actually," Doc corrected without seeming to do so.

Jack ran a hand through his mop of dishwater blond hair tinged with copper. "Eventful," he replied. "But successful."

"Some kind of stone, eh?" Edison wondered. "Would've liked to examine that."

Jack jettisoned an uncomfortable look by clearing his throat. "We, uh...we made the call in the field, sir. The artifact belongs to the Aymara. But they've given us an open invitation to study the *camasca* stone there, on-site."

"As long as we're respectful," Doc added.

Edison cast a look at the couple, suddenly quite solemn. "The Silver Star will try to take it again. Crowley will stop at nothing. You do know that."

"We do," Jack nodded in the affirmative. "And we have forces stationed close by in case they do make another attempt."

"If you mean those sky pirates..." Edison scoffed, letting a sarcastic chuckle escape his throat.

Jack's brow furrowed. "Stede Bonnet is a war hero and an ace pilot, Mr. Edison."

"And Bonnet's Brigands aren't our only allies in the region," Doc explained, trying to soothe the tension between her hot-headed idealist partner and her elderly patron. "Colonel Shaw has been putting together special units across the globe." She looked over her shoulder at Deadeye. "The...what was it? *Defensores?*"

"*Defensores de la Tierra Dorada...*or just DTD," Deadeye confirmed.

"I like *Defensores,*" Sparks opined from the corner of the room, where she perused the latest copy of *Life* magazine.

Doc returned her gaze to Edison. "They'll be watching all of Latin America."

Edison waved a hand in dismissal. "Ehh. Shaw's infatuation with vigilantes and mystery men will put us at a disadvantage. Mark my words."

Jack threw Doc a sidelong look, and she nodded back.

"Give us a minute?" she asked.

Sarah ushered the crew silently toward the exit, and Jack gave Doc's shoulder a supportive touch before following them out. Doc had been Edison's chief headhunter in the early days of AEGIS, the architect of much of its success. They had history together, the shared loss of Doc's husband, and an emotional shorthand. The inventor had a mercurial temperament, and Dorothy Starr knew how to navigate the shoals and eddies.

When the door had shut, Doc found Edison's eyes and locked with them. "What is it, Mr. Edison? Really?" They were long past the point of addressing each other by last names, and he certainly didn't with her, but Doc still held the man in high regard, as a man of science and a mentor.

Edison reached into his breast pocket, producing a handkerchief and honking into it like a goose. "I'm sorry, Dorothy. I really am pleased to see you." Shoving the hanky into his side pocket, he turned to gesture at the pile of reference materials and reports on his desk. "I've just been having trouble keeping up with the growth of the organization. Not as young as I used to be, you know."

"None of us are, sir," Doc replied. "And you're pretty darn spry for a man of your years."

"Ha!" Edison erupted with a single laugh. "My years are fast coming to a close, and you are a terrible liar." His old eyes glanced up to meet hers. "But it makes me smile, so you keep right on lying."

Doc displayed a pained look. "Is there anything I might do?"

"That you aren't already doing?" he asked rhetorically. "No. Just keep taking care of that crew of yours. And that family."

"Yes sir."

"That little girl," Edison muttered, nodding toward the office door. "Ellen? She's the spitting image of you and Jack. Gonna make a hell of a field agent one day."

Doc blushed. "If she does, it'll be her father's influence. She gets all of her risk-taking tendencies from him."

They shared a brief laugh, then the room fell silent. Edison found Doc's eyes with serious intent. "Dorothy, out of every damn one of the people working with AEGIS, I trust you the most. To do the hard work. To make the hard choices. Because I know you're doing it to keep your family safe, to make the world better for your daughter's generation. Don't ever lose sight of that."

Doc blushed and cast her gaze at the floor. "I won't, sir."

"Someday," Edison sighed, "you'll be running this operation."

Doc froze in place. "You can't mean that, sir. Your partners, Mr. Ford and Mr. Firestone, and the other financial backers..."

"Ehh," Edison repeated, waving a dismissive hand once again. "Anybody can make a product people want to buy. Anybody can make a buck." He pawed through a stack of papers in an open file folder on the desk, fishing out an official-looking form. "But you know *people*, and you know the *occult*, and you know the *enemy*. You know how to walk in many worlds simultaneously. And that makes you of more practical use than the longer-lasting light bulb."

He returned to Doc and handed her the paper from the file.

"What's this?" she wondered aloud, peering at the type.

"New assignment," the old inventor explained. "Last one this year, I promise. I know you'd rather be back at the ranch." He referred to the property in southern California she shared with Jack and Ellen.

Doc sighed. He wasn't wrong about that. She missed the slower pace of life at the ranch. Jack working with his hired mechanic, Jinx, sweating over some engine, repairing the fence, or harvesting walnuts in the orchard. Leisurely family dinners. Lounging by the swimming pool while quizzing Ellen on her homework.

Edison continued: "But Bill Boeing has something he wants to try out on the LR-3s and your crew is the most familiar with them. I trust you folks to handle it."

"Boeing? I wonder what it could be..." She folded the orders and slipped them into her jacket pocket.

"I told him if it was an offensive weapon, I didn't want to know. So, he didn't say," Edison shrugged. "You're expected in Seattle by the end of the week. Bill's people will have more for you then."

"Alright," Doc said. "We'll get it done." She took Edison's hands and added softly, "And you take care of yourself, Tom." Leaning in toward his cheek, she left a friendly kiss and then broke away, ambling toward the study door. "Please give Mina my love—"

"Give Bill my best," Edison interrupted, having not heard her own comment.

It shouldn't have shocked her as much as she let it appear. Nodding with a sad smile, Doc exited the room.

When the door had shut once more, the old man took a deep breath through flared nostrils, sighing audibly. He didn't think he was out of touch, but recently found himself increasingly at sea when it came to AEGIS operations and the ever-escalating threat of the Silver Star.

He knew in his gut that Crowley was planning something, something inconceivably monstrous in both scale and effect. He wished he knew precisely what, so he could better prepare the brave men and women of the AEGIS organization, for they would carry on the vital work of defending the innocent when he was gone. At least he hoped they would.

Leaning forward on the desk with one hand, he reached up to massage a pair of tired eyes with the other. "Godspeed, *Daedalus*."

- CHAPTER 6 -

Maria Blutig stepped tentatively across the ice, her boot disturbing only the slightest amount of snow from the overnight accumulation. The vibrations were strongest here.

Scanning the horizon back toward the mountainous shoreline of northern Greenland, she could see the line of white-clad Arctic troopers assembled a few paces beyond, automatic rifles slung as they awaited further orders. The summer melt was upon the region, and the expanse of frozen sea on which she carefully tread was rent with fissures and canyons. The surface was a prism of glistening diamond points in the endless summer day.

She knew it would be necessary to move with all due speed.

She found the edge of the giant floe, where the white ice met an isolated pool of open sea.

Reaching outward with her senses, she plunged them down, like a camera on a long cable. Down through the ice and into the darkness below, into the freezing deep, where the burnt hulk of a Norwegian tall ship now lay in sundered pieces on the sea floor. She saw in her mind's eye the corpses scattered between planks and rocks, the bodies in various stages of decay—people who had once been Nordic sailors, or Inuit hunters, or even a Viking descendant from a lost enclave living in a thermal valley. People who had in death been resurrected by a powerful eldritch pulse from an alien beacon.

A beacon which Captain Hummel had been sent to retrieve for the Silver Star. A beacon the *Daedalus* crew had stolen from his very hand as he dropped into the cold blackness to his death.

And there he was.

His frozen body, blue and shriveled, lay at the prow of the old ship, formerly dark hair now stripped of pigment and wafting in the mild current. His white parka had darkened to the color of his charcoal officer's uniform, shiny leather knee boots now dull and soft-ened by sea water.

Captain Ernst Hummel, the *Schwarzhund*, or Black Dog of the Baltic during the Great War, commander of the Silver Star supercarri-er *Osiris*. A slowly-decomposing corpse on the floor of the Arctic Ocean.

But Maria yet had plans for Captain Hum-mel.

Sinking to her knees on the shimmering ice, she thrust her palms out, then down, fin-gers spread intensely as if playing the opening chords of a Beethoven symphony. She needed no spoken words, no arcane recitation to en-tice the natural order to do her bidding. Her power came from sheer will alone.

As the fingers of her left hand pressed and plucked at the cold air, the palm of her right suddenly shot up into the air above her head. A phosphorescent green pulse exploded from her body in a complete sphere, causing a shockwave a hundred meters away. Several of the armed soldiers at the shoreline staggered in place at the atmospheric punch.

The pulse dissipated as soon as it erupted, the glowing green orb expanding to nothing-ness within a couple of hundred meters.

Maria slumped forward, drained of mystical energy. Her hands pressed down into the soft, frozen powder atop the ice.

"Rise," she commanded, from deep in her throat. "Rise."

As the assembled soldiers watched, the sea under Maria's kneeling form began to emit that same emerald glow. It gradually spread beneath her, growing and expanding like a bonfire, illuminating the ice like an aquatic aurora. Black silhouettes began to drift up, from the shipwreck below, through the light.

Bony, talon-like hands broke the surface of the water, clawing at the edge of the ice. Limbs clambered onto the solid surface where, despite the season, their old, saturated clothes immediately developed an icy crust.

"Rise, my darlings," Maria breathed in guttural sighs. "All of you."

Staggering to her feet, she stepped forward, approaching the water's edge as skeletal body after body began to crawl from the depths onto the floe. At last, a dozen resurrected corpses stood in the Arctic summer breeze, swaying in place, awaiting her command. Their eyes were a field of eerie green stars. The tallest of the ghouls was a blond, bearded man in furs, whose body cavity had been stripped of internal organs, half its head blown away by the exit of a rifle round. Maria did not know who the man had been in life, but she could sense a connection with her old enemies, the *Daedalus* crew. He peered blankly with those green, glowing ember eyes.

The shuffling sound of boots scraping on snow came from the middle of the crowd, and the grotesque approximation of the man who'd once been the Black Dog of the Silver Star staggered to the front. He said nothing, but stared at Maria out of gelatinous eyes that emitted that same emerald light.

Maria smiled sadly at Hummel, or what was left of him. There was perhaps some pity within her for his plight. "Come, *Kapitän*," she said in an almost motherly tone. "There is much to do."

From the line of assembled troops along the shoreline, Captain Jonas Ecke surveyed the scene, watching the play of unearthly green light under the ice like an aquatic aurora. A veteran of the Great War, Ecke had commanded Zeppelin bombers for the Central Powers. He'd laid waste to half of London and demolished French industrial targets without ever having lost a ship. After the war, he'd been offered a post commanding the flagship of Aleister Crowley's paramilitary army, the *Luftpanzer,* a massive super-zeppelin. When that airship had been destroyed by AEGIS field agents while at anchor in the Amazon, a new supercarrier had been deployed in its place, the *Luftpanzer II*. But although he was still in practical command of the replacement, it was often Maria Blutig given operational control of various missions, leaving Ecke a glorified chauffeur. And an ever more frustrated one with each passing assignment.

He'd witnessed in amazement the supernatural feats Maria was able to execute. The illusory camouflage she used to make an entire airship "disappear". The absorption of an individual's life force to replenish and augment her own. He'd watched her raise a small army of the dead from an Amazonian swamp, using them as rocket-propelled soldiers against her most hated enemy, the *Daedalus* crew. He'd seen her in victory and in defeat, and much preferred victory. He knew Maria to be insecure, vindictive, and ambitious in the extreme, so he'd never made the mistake of crossing her.

But now, yet again, he was assigned to command the *Osiris* in a two-pronged assault on that old enemy. The *Luftpanzer II* was docked in an undisclosed location in the far east, undergoing a major refit. So not only was Ecke simply shifted like a chess piece to a role Crowley saw as interchangeable, The Great

Beast of Mankind had the temerity to call it a "promotion".

The more he learned about the actual operation, the less optimistic he felt about it. But he knew better than to complain. Although he'd been recruited in the early days of the *Astrum Argentum*, without the requirement of the Soul Contract, Ecke was still mortal, and he knew Crowley had absolutely no compunctions about executing someone for any reason that benefited him.

No, Captain Jonas Ecke would stay the course, command the crew of the *Osiris*, and see this mission through to the end—wherever that end would lead him.

༄

The townhouse on Green Street stood dark and silent against the London night. A visitor might have presumed the home to be uninhabited, without realizing both the darkness and silence were the result of a magical construct. Beneath the protective veil, work proceeded apace. Armed commandos stood ready to strike from the shadows, and four snipers occupied the slate roof, each covering a quarter of the compass.

Within the building, acolytes scurried from assignment to assignment, unquestioning. The music study had been cleared of the grand piano which used to assume the lion's share of the large circular space. The array of glass panes encircling the room looked out toward the back garden, though at present they were obscured under endless black drapery.

The conservatory walls seemed to warp and shimmer as the air distorted in front of the two men. Both clad in ceremonial robes of black and red, the taller of the two held his right hand aloft, as if conducting some kind of cosmic orchestra.

"I call upon the guardians of space and time,

To hear my solemn query;

To bear witness to this ethereal rhyme,

And slake not thy fury..."

The chant rose up from the robed form with hand held high, once-resonant English baritone now nasally and almost cartoonish in timbre.

"Master! It is working!" erupted slavishly from the smaller man, in an almost identical accent.

As they watched, a welt began to form in the air in front of them, a vertical aperture like the eye of a reptile. It swelled and ultimately tore open, revealing one of the agents recently assigned to AEGIS headquarters. The man wore a black overcoat and matching Stetson fedora, eyes squinting against the bright illumination pouring forth from his side of the rift.

"M-258," Crowley addressed. "Come forth and deliver your quarry."

Stepping forward without hesitation, the agent reached back into the vortex, his outstretched hand clutching a leather pouch of glass vials. As he did so, a shock ran through his body, and he felt his hand begin to burn. The skin crisped and dropped away like charred ash from a fireplace log. The agent knew that if he succumbed to the pain and cried out, odds were high that the Master would call due his Soul Contract. His jaw set, teeth clamped shut, the agent silently extended his arm through the hole in time and space, dropping the case and withdrawing quickly. But instead of a human appendage returning, he saw that the arm he pulled out was a soft coil of multiple stalks, like the tentacles of a cephalopod. The image through the rift grew momentarily brighter and then went completely black.

The smaller robed man in the darkened conservatory caught the case in midair and marveled at the magic that had just transpired.

A tiny roll of thunder echoed through the cavernous room.

Crowley turned away from the closed rift, directing his acolyte to a purpose-built stone altar where the piano once stood. A silver bowl and various spell components lay strewn across the linen drapery covering the altar's surface. "Bring the samples," he instructed. "Bring them now."

The acolyte hurried to his master's side, offering the black leather case. As he watched, the Master took a handful of sculpting clay about the size of a baseball from the table and placed it in the bowl. Then he slid the vials from the case and methodically emptied the contents of each one over the lump of artist's medium, chanting:

> *"Like the Hebrew magus of antiquity,*
>
> *I call upon the spirit of the golem;*
>
> *Take ye the form of those whose blood*
>
> *Ye now absorb..."*

The crimson contents of the glass vials splattered and pooled over the clay, soaking into the mass. Crowley then opened another, separate vial which had been resting on its side among the other spell components. This, too, was emptied onto the clay. Lastly, he sprinkled in a pinch of some kind of dried fungus the shade of aquamarine.

"Rise, *homunculus*," he instructed to the dark lump of clay. "Rise and do my will upon the Earth." He held his right hand over the bowl, his palm emitting the briefest arc of blue-white electricity.

As Cowley and his acolyte observed, the clay began to spasm and pulsate. It stretched vertically, like a finger reaching toward the ceiling, and gradually began to swell and twist itself into the general proportions of a tiny humanoid. Rudimentary limbs sprouted from the center, streaked with the blood and fungus mixture. It stood on two diminutive legs, its gray color saturated dark red and appearing almost jet black as a result.

The acolyte stepped back with a gasp. He was doing it. Crowley was creating life...of sorts.

The master occultist leaned down over the small figure. A single eye blinked open, perhaps the size of a walnut. "I will see what you see," Crowley informed the tiny figure. "And you shall obey my commands."

Yes, Crowley thought. *This will do nicely. It will make them doubt, and where there is doubt soon follows fear. This will allow me to strike deep at very heart of AEGIS.*

He cast a backward look over his shoulder to his robed servant. "Prepare a new portal."

- CHAPTER 7 -

After the long journey from Peru, Jack ordered his crew to take it easy for a couple of days while they were cleared of any sign of tropical infection. While the *Daedalus* was repaired and re-provisioned, Jack and Doc spent a quiet couple of nights at the home of Doc's aunts, Millie and Agnes Brown, outside of Newark. Ten-year-old Ellen Starr was elated to be reunited with her parents and kept asking when they could get back to the ranch in southern California.

When the answer wasn't forthcoming, she made a convincing pre-teen argument to tag along on the trip to Seattle, seeing as how the crew was one short. She furthermore asserted that she'd been flying her dad's planes for the past three years, and therefore could handle herself in the air "like a real pro".

Doc knew she was likely bored with her studies under the tutelage of the Brown sisters, despite their loving and progressive instruction. Ellen had a disproportionate amount of Jack's risk-taking genetic makeup, and definitely preferred flying planes or racing motorcycles through Quigley Canyon and the Santa Clarita Valley, or trail riding with western movie star William S. Hart, whose ranch abutted their own. Both Jack and Doc assumed this would be a routine test of some new mechanical system. It seemed like an easy proposal to say yes to.

When Ellen rested her case by proclaiming that she even traveled with her own Beeman's spearmint gum to equalize her eardrums while in the air, producing the white pack from her pinafore dress as proof, Jack had to admit he was convinced.

"Sold!" he asserted, before offering his daughter a field commission at the rank of "Junior Aeronaut". Nothing that would require official paperwork in triplicate, but which would satisfy a precocious young girl's fantasy of standing side-by-side with the grownups. It was too short notice to have a uniform custom-made, and nothing in her size could be requisitioned from the AEGIS Quartermaster. She'd have to make do with bib overalls and a blue cotton pullover she used for various outdoor sporting activities. Jack did give her one of his two lapel pins that displayed the AEGIS winged shield and sword insignia, sticking it through the sweater collar and securing it with the butterfly clutch in back.

Their number back up to six, well-rested and well-fed after two days' furlough, the crew assembled on the tarmac at Kenilworth, each performing a safety walkaround of the airship prior to launch. She'd been patched, painted and polished, stress-points reinforced and worn-out dynamos replaced.

Sparks entered through the cargo bay and noted the three gyro-packs they usually carried had been removed. In their place was an identical number of smaller devices resembling a rigid knapsack with a pair of canister vacuums welded on. Each pack was secured to a wall hook which also supported a light crash helmet.

A wire-bound technical manual which smelled of fresh mimeograph ink lay closed on the Master Control desk in the engine room. Apparently the old gyro-packs were being phased out in favor of AEGIS' in-house development of the JP10 jetpack. Interesting, as she was unaware of any *Daedalus* crewmembers actually being trained on the brand-new technology. She'd have to bring this up with the captain at some point. But now was not the time.

Jack slid into the pilot's seat and strapped the safety harness across his chest. The *Daedalus* was released from the mooring cleats at Kenilworth, drifting into the summer morning sky as the massive thrust engines powered on.

Rail travelers could take the Transcontinental Express from New York to San Francisco in about four days. The LR3 series airship took Jack McGraw and his crew from West Orange, New Jersey to Seattle, Washington in just over twenty-four hours, despite more than one headwind and a route adjustment to avoid a thunderstorm over the Dakotas.

Four-hour duty watches on the bridge were made far more bearable by way of Cipher piping radio broadcasts over the comms. There seemed to be exponentially more stations than this time last year, and many of them featured popular music played by live bands and orchestras.

Threading a low-pressure corridor, the *Daedalus* came in over Portland, Oregon just after sunrise, crossing the Columbia River in a wide right turn. The landscape was tinged in hues of pink and orange. Verdant forests and farmlands lay strewn beneath them, cradled between the Olympic and Cascade mountain ranges. Jack had flown the region just two years prior, as part of the shakedown cruise of this very airship. When weather was mild, as it was today, the scenery couldn't be beat. Majestic volcanic mountains like St. Helens and Rainier—*Tahoma* to the indigenous Coast Salish tribes—were sentinels of the primeval beauty that beckoned visitors like the sirens of Greek myth. To the west, the Olympics sprouted like gnarled white teeth from a thick, green, ancient forest. Olympia's stately capitol dome shone in the early sunlight from its seat at the bottom corner of Puget Sound.

Charting a northerly course between the volcanoes to the east and the island-strewn waters to the west, Jack made their final approach beyond the port city of Tacoma to an airfield larger than any he'd ever seen in this part of the country. Circling high above Boeing Field, with its long runways, single terminal, and various hangars and support facilities, he waited for Cipher to secure landing clearance. Within fifteen minutes, they were cleating down near the mechanics' shop. A crowd began to form almost immediately, some of the early shift workers applauding as the sleek dirigible was locked in place and the crew disembarked. Hands were shaken, autographs signed. Airplane mechanics and technicians gawped at the 200-foot chrome envelope, pointing and laying tentative fingers on the mammoth thrust engine housings.

Boeing Field had just been dedicated the previous year, and it was as shiny and modern an airfield as any on the west coast. Centrally located between the ports of Seattle and Tacoma, it boasted plenty of open field for north or south approaches, and a state-of-the-art control tower to boot.

A slender fellow of average stature, smartly dressed in a gray three-piece suit, pushed to the front of the crowd. He wore round spectacles and a black felt bowler, with a shaved dome beneath. An impeccably-trimmed black mustache spread across his upper lip, frosted with white.

Jack and Doc both turned to acknowledge the newcomer as he doffed his hat, clearly excited to be in the presence of international heroes yet maintaining a facade of stoic calm.

"Captain Stratosphere?" the man addressed. "Er, Captain McGraw?"

The two men fumbled between a salute and a handshake for a brief moment, ultimately deciding on the latter. Even so, Jack McGraw could tell a military bearing on a man.

"Call me Jack," he answered. "This is Doc." He gestured back and forth between crewmembers. "Deadeye, Cipher, Sparks, and Junior Aeronaut Ellen Starr."

"Callsign Red." Ellen thrust her hand out, and the man shook it warmly, adding a bewildered smile.

"Robert MacLennan," he said, nodding at the assembled party. "No callsign, Royal Canadian Mounted Police. I'm your liaison with the Canadian government."

Jack and Doc exchanged a look.

"Canadian government?" Jack squinted. "I thought we were testing the new gear out here over the Puget Sound..."

"That was the initial plan, yes," MacLennan explained. "But if you check with AEGIS Command, they'll confirm the change of mission parameters. They wanted a less-populated area for the testing."

"Less-populated?" Doc exclaimed, "what are they installing?"

MacLennan's face fell. "Oh dear. You haven't been told?"

"I assumed it was some kind of weapon," Jack said. "What with Edison not wanting to talk about it."

"Let's take a walk to the mechanics' hangar, shall we?" MacLennan nodded toward the large workshop nearby, and the crew followed. Wide barn doors were open to the pleasant morning air, and acetylene overhead lamps illuminated the cavernous interior. Workers in worn gray coveralls scurried to and fro on various tasks and errands. An occasional eruption of sparks from the odd welding torch added a flicker of light to the faces of the gathered airship crew.

MacLennan found a work desk and produced a folded paper from his inside breast pocket. He lay it out on the flat surface, unfolding it to its proper original size. Jack could see immediately that it was a technical schematic of some kind of weapon system.

"It's an air-to-air torpedo," MacLennan revealed. "Goes up front, under the bridge. They'll remove the forward guns and graft the launch device over the turret canopy..."

"Ah, MacLennan! You're here!" hailed a voice from the bright world outside the shop. "Good deal!"

Doc turned to see another man approaching from the light. He eventually became recognizable.

Robert MacLennan and Bill Boeing could have been brothers in terms of stature and facial features, right down to fashion choices. Boeing had the distinction of a short haircut, slicked to one side with pomade, but otherwise matched MacLennan in his round specs and frosted mustache. He was a middle-aged man of German extraction, his face affixed with an enigmatic semi-smile that approximated the Mona Lisa.

"Mr. Boeing," MacLennan greeted. "This is the crew of the AEGIS airship *Daedalus...*"

As he approached, looking over the crew, Boeing's smile fell and his demeanor shifted to one of personal discomfort. Half of the faces assembled were of a darker complexion than Boeing was used to dealing with, and his nose screwed up despite itself.

Doc noticed. "I hope there's no problem?"

"Uh, no," Boeing replied, clearing his throat. "But...I asked AEGIS for their best and brightest, and this is—"

Before he could finish with, "—this is what they send me," Jack interrupted, finishing it for him.

"This *is* the best and brightest, Mr. Boeing," he retorted, looming over the airplane designer in the stark light of the shop. "In AEGIS or anywhere else in the world, for that matter." Jack knew they didn't need a champion to ride in on a white steed and defend them as individuals, but they were also his crew, his family. And they'd been insulted.

He knew from experience it was better to address matters of personal prejudice quickly and openly, instead of sweeping them under the carpet. The crew were well aware that they could speak up at any time on their own behalf, yet it was equally important for a commander in the field to advocate for his or her team members.

Boeing opened his mouth to say something, but Jack cut him off. "Each of them has saved my life, and whether you know it or not, *yours,* more than once." His voice dropped an octave and Doc wondered if her partner was about to challenge the other man to a duel. "So show some damn respect."

Sparks and Deadeye caught a look from each other and stifled a chuckle. Cipher pursed her lips to contain her own smile.

Jack turned away from Boeing in a pantomime of disdain, leaving the airplane magnate to stare in open-mouthed confusion. He found the eyes of each of his crew, gauging their reaction. All nodded in reply, winking or rolling their eyes in disbelief that Boeing had voiced such a provincial personal bias out loud. His look and tone had made his feelings perfectly clear.

Truth be told, McGraw had had enough of the so-called captains of industry being treated like precious works of art, coddled by the government, lionized in the press, and worshiped by the public. His friendship with Edison had reinforced the reality that they were just people, like anyone else, complex and flawed. He knew with the supreme confidence of experience that his crew was in fact the best field team in all of AEGIS, and that Boeing needed them more than they needed him *and* whatever pea-shooter he wanted to graft onto their ship. AEGIS was doing him a favor, letting their vehicle be the guinea pig for a new weapon system in exchange for leveraging, and purchasing units of, that technology.

Boeing stood frozen in place, eyes darting furtively. "I..." he muttered. "I spoke in haste. My apologies." Then he nodded at MacLennan and indicated the blueprint on the desk. "I trust you have this all in order? Call my office if you need anything. Anything at all." Giving a nervous half-bow to the crew, he added, "It was nice meeting you all. Best of luck." And then he disappeared into the bright haze out-side.

Jack and Doc exchanged a look and sighed in unison. Everyone turned their attention to MacLennan, who shrugged at Boeing's strange behavior, visibly uncomfortable at its subject matter.

"Well then," he said, clearing his throat. "Let's go over the weapon system and mission parameters, shall we?"

- CHAPTER 8 -

Colonel Stephen Shaw glanced up from the open file on his desk. His face was angular, features chiseled and clean-shaven. A black leather patch covered his left orbital socket, while his right eye shone blue-gray in the soft falloff from the desk lamp. He spoke in a posh, measured tone, though his expression was one of alarm. "Is this intelligence correct?"

The woman standing across the table from Shaw was a silhouette with eyes—two points of amber piercing Todd haze of the tiny office. A long leather coat and hooded mantle bulked up an otherwise lithe frame, and an un-adorned wool *šajkača* hat sat cocked over a mane of coal black hair.

"I watch them myself," she said quietly, in a thick Slavic accent.

Shaw leaned back from the desk, a winged shield and sword lapel pin now glinting in the cone of light. "Crowley back in England...good God. And you say they're up to something?"

The silhouette shifted. "People go in, they do not ever come out."

"I don't understand," Shaw protested. "I've had that residence in Mayfair under observation for months. Not one report of any activity."

"Your people cannot penetrate the veil," the woman answered. "He fools all with powerful magicks, which lie to the eyes." The silhouette moved forward silently and for the first time, the woman's face lowered into view. She was dark-complected, her features almost Indian, gold-brown eyes outlined in smoky black cosmetic shadow. "I have the Sight. Like my mother and grandmother before me. Is Roma gift."

Shaw leaned into the desk light, matching her gesture. "Mila, if you're correct, we have to do this very carefully."

"I don't care how you do it," the mysterious woman replied, venom in her words. "My people fought in the Great War. We served the Kingdom of Serbia and were slaughtered for our trouble. Those who survived the war were driven deep into the wilderness—but we are Roma! We make new homes there! Then came Crowley with his thugs and his sky-ship. The Silver Star destroyed my clan. Took my brother for sacrifice." Her eyes widened, cheeks flushed with a controlled rage that made Colonel Shaw's heart skip.

"Mila..." he began.

But she wasn't finished. "Colonel Shaw, I have tracked and watched them for seven years. I do not mind a few days more." She stood straight again, her face disappearing into the dark office corner, yet her eyes remained visible. "So long as I am there when you go in. I will have my revenge, one way or another. In this life, or the next."

"Agreed," Shaw answered earnestly. "Mila, I want Crowley as much as you. We have all manner of arrest warrants and court orders forbidding him entry to Britain. But we will need special people to carry out an operation like this—people who can see as you do. Through the veil, as it were."

Shaw stood from his chair, pressing out the front of his double-breasted suit as he did so. He peered across the darkened office at the silhouette he called Mila. His single eye found her two.

"Yes," he muttered under his breath. "Yes, it's time."

As Mila watched from the shadows, Colonel Shaw plucked the candlestick telephone from his desk, holding the earpiece to his right ear and thumbing the cradle as he spoke into the round microphone at the top. "Yes, Imelda? Ring Paris, will you? I need Joe Desmond."

❧

"It's ugly."

Sparks surveyed the twin torpedo launch tubes which now sprouted about four feet proud of the forward gun turret. The entire weapon resembled the double barrels of an oversized shotgun, with the primitive electronics housed within the turret's protective carapace.

The motors which normally drove the gunnery station's movements had been disconnected, giving the new weapon a firing arc of precisely zero degrees. How the hell were they supposed to hit anything with it? Sparks clucked her tongue at the monstrosity and shook her head. A weapon system that required absolute precision facing from a dirigible in the air didn't seem very practical, to say the least.

She gave Deadeye a bewildered look, and the marksman shrugged.

But then as mechanics and electricians began tearing up Doc's navigation console on the bridge, MacLennan explained that precise facing wouldn't be necessary at all. The weapon's rocket projectiles would be guided by a radio signal, allowing for almost infinite course correction while in flight.

Doc looked on in horror as her bridge station was completely reconfigured. "Where is navigation to be?" she worried.

"Looks like the proving grounds are a straight shot north," Jack offered, scanning an open chart on MacLennan's workshop table. "Along the western coast of British Columbia."

"Correct," MacLennan nodded, pointing a slender finger to a point on the map. "We're actually headed to an outpost on the Sunshine Coast, at the western end of an inlet of Howe Sound. Mostly small timber and mining communities...no real population center. We should have the Strait of Georgia mostly to ourselves."

Jack found Doc's hand and squeezed it gently. "We can make do with the chart room for the time being," he said. "You'll have your nav station back before we head home."

Doc's furrowed brow met his, and they shared a silent moment that nonetheless communicated volumes. She didn't like this. They weren't a research and development team. They were a front-line field operations crew. Jack was used to testing new technology, whether it be a weapon or the machine that carried it. But he understood the hesitation among his crew. This mission was not the type they were typically used to.

As they broke away, Jack spoke to Doc in soft tones. "Hey, we'll be finished within a couple, three days."

Doc looked skeptical.

"A week, tops," he amended.

Ellen watched her parents' exchange from atop a stool near the worktable, jawing a piece of Beeman's spearmint gum. They did this a lot, talking cryptically and in fragments. She trusted it.

Saying nothing, Doc turned and left the hangar, meandering into the sunlight outside.

She found Cipher watching a work crew as they went over a new model of the Boeing 80 airliner. The 80A had more passenger space and hauling capacity, and would be undergoing its maiden flight in just three weeks.

"She's pretty," Doc noted, indicating the large biplane on the tarmac.

Cipher shifted her attention with her weight. "More commercial air travel," she said, in her posh received pronunciation. "If someone perfects a practical jet engine, it means transcontinental flights in less than a day."

Doc exhaled a sigh, impressed. "Whew. Not even rail can do that. Not even the *Daedalus* can do that. We can do thirty hours only because we stand watches and don't have to stop for fuel."

"The skies will be full," Cipher predicted.

Doc agreed. "Getting fuller by the day already."

Without pausing, Cipher handed Doc a folded telegram.

"What's this?" Doc frowned, unfolding the yellow paper. It bore the letterhead of the Boeing Airplane & Transport Corporation, which meant the transmission had come directly to the airfield, as opposed to the local Western Union office. Looking over its contents, Doc could see the familiar jumble of seemingly random letters and numbers. It was in code. "Cipher, I don't—"

"I'm sorry, ma'am," Cipher offered. "I forget most people don't simply decode on the fly." Her brown eyes remained unblinking on the

80A prototype before her, its fabric-covered duralumin frame gleaming in the sunlight as technicians continued the inspection process. "It's from AEGIS Command," she explained. "As soon as we're done with the weapons testing, they want me back at Kenilworth."

Doc raised an eyebrow, equal parts apprehensive and intrigued. "For what reason?" she asked.

Cipher closed her eyes, a smile spreading gradually. "They've offered me command of the *Vayu*."

"The *Vayu*?" Doc's eyes widened. She knew the *Vayu* was one of three LR3 airships deployed on the heels of the *Daedalus* and *Percival* in late 1927, the other two being the *Achilles* and the *Cerberus*. "That's...why, that's amazing!" Then she recalled something and her brow furrowed again. "But isn't the *Vayu* under the command of..."

"Commander Man Mohan Singh," Cipher answered preemptively. "A distant cousin. He named the ship after the Hindu lord of the winds." She shifted her weight again, turning to face Doc. "Apparently, he's leaving AEGIS to help launch India's aviation industry. They offered me his commission."

"That's just wonderful," Doc beamed, grabbing the younger woman in a congratulatory hug. "I don't know what to say!"

They parted, and Cipher gave Doc a serious look. "Good. Don't mention it to the captain," she implored. "Not for the time being, anyway. I don't want him distracted with my departure."

"That's a hard secret to keep," Doc worried. "But I'll do my damnedest." They momentarily caught each other's gaze and broke out into smiles. "And congratulations, *Commander* Singh!"

In the shade of the workshop, there was precious little more to be done, by Jack or anyone else. While Bill Boeing's technical crew assembled the wiring harnesses and bridge controls into what would become known as the Operations Station on the bridge, the *Daedalus* crew enjoyed a night out in Seattle. A movie at the Paramount, dinner at The Athenian at Pike Place Market, and overnight accommodations at the upscale Benjamin Franklin Hotel, which had just opened in February.

Throughout the evening, Doc and Cipher exchanged knowing looks and surreptitious smiles, with nobody the wiser. Jack was just happy to have his crew together, and his daughter with them. Ellen was pleased to be in adult company who didn't fawn over her every comment, and who let her participate in their conversations.

The crew assembled at Boeing Field early the following morning, in field dress, ready to begin their assigned mission. The AEGIS LR3 airship waited in the morning sunlight, cleated to the ground with aluminum cables.

There was a short briefing: MacLennan would fly separately in a support craft, an older Boeing PB-1 flying boat, which would carry the actual munitions and extra supplies for the weapons test. They would rendezvous at a small trading village at the mouth of Howe Sound called Gibsons Landing. The RCMP had an outpost there, which would function as the mission base camp and headquarters. Allowing for present weather conditions, flight time to destination was approximately two hours. Once there, the crew would be given an orientation of the facilities and a further briefing for the testing schedule. Canadian military surplus gliders and mothballed fishing vessels would provide the targets, all unmanned, of course.

After two days of targeting and guidance testing, the crew would make a field report, MacLennan would make his own report to the

Canadian government, and the *Daedalus* would head back to Seattle for refitting. *And then*, Jack and Ellen both thought, *back home to Newhall, to fly Quigley Canyon in the Fleetwing again!*

Doc just hoped for some quiet study time.

"Easy as pie," Jack quipped, winding his index finger in the air. "Okay, crew! Let's saddle up!"

- CHAPTER 9 -

The flight took them across the entirety of Puget Sound from south to north. Islands both large and small scattered like jigsaw puzzle pieces on a blue-green carpet. To the east of them, the city of Seattle bustled with commerce. To the west, the Olympic forest and mountain range caught the morning light, a stippled golden shawl across an almost endless sea of deep green forest.

In the main saloon, Deadeye, Sparks, and Ellen shared morning beverages around the table closest to the starboard windows. On the bridge, Cipher manned the radio console as usual, while Jack pushed the airship ever northward from the helm.

Doc leaned over the left side of the pilot's chair, resting a delicate hand on Jack's collar. She kept glancing back over her shoulder at the former navigation console, now conspicuously called Operations, at least for the time being.

Jack noticed and found it distracting. He decided to address it openly. "It's temporary," he asserted in a gravelly tone.

"I know," Doc sighed, "I know." She gave Jack's shoulder a gentle squeeze. "I just...I don't feel good about this."

Jack squinted through the forward windscreens. A pod of orca whales followed the same course, dorsal fins standing tall from the water. "Look," he offered, "why don't you and Ellen go ashore when we get to Gibsons Landing? She shouldn't be aboard for the active weapons test anyway, and you don't need to learn yet *another* bridge officer job. Deadeye can handle the operations console."

"You sure?" Doc asked, a skeptical tone creeping in.

"I'm sure," Jack affirmed. "It's a cakewalk." He turned to give Doc a sly wink. "Just try not to get in too much trouble around those Mounties. I know how you love a man in uniform."

Doc gave a throaty laugh. "Why, Captain," she said, squeezing his shoulder a second time, "there's only one man I'm interested in, uniform or no." She leaned over to his left ear and whispered, "In fact he looks best in nothing at all."

"MacLennan just radioed," Cipher announced, deftly tuning a knob on the receiver. "XPB-1 has takeoff from Elliott Bay."

Jack cleared his throat, blushing from Doc's comment. "They should be catching up with us pretty soon."

"It'll be nice to have an escort in," Doc offered. "Y'know, since we don't have a nav station anymore."

Jack rolled his eyes, pretending to ignore the complaint. Within ten minutes, a shadow fell across the nose of the *Daedalus*, and MacLennan's flying boat gradually passed overhead. Jack estimated its speed somewhere between five and ten miles per hour faster than that of the airship, as it dropped into the lead several hundred meters ahead and maintained the distance.

The odd pair of aircraft followed the coastline northward, making a twenty-degree left turn as they passed over the sleepy Washington town of Bellingham. Below, a flotilla of fishing boats spread out into the shimmering waters of Bellingham Bay, on the prowl for the day's salmon catch.

Just a few more miles ahead, the Strait of Georgia and Boundary Bay represented the northern U.S. border with Canada, a single body of water with two official names. A series of political agreements between the two allied nations artificially bisected land and sea alike, and the residents on each side went on with their lives. Despite the southern fifth of Vancouver Island dipping well below the 49th parallel and the American enclave of Point Roberts sitting isolated at the tip of the Tsawwassen Peninsula in British Columbia, a century of diplomacy had forged what was now the longest international border in the world, and one without an active military defense on either side.

Another half hour put them over Vancouver, already a bustling metropolis not three decades into the new century, as modern as any city in the industrial world. But just outside of its modest urban sprawl extended a seemingly eternal blanket of deep green. Forests of lodgepole pine, red cedar, white spruce, and subalpine fir merged with the fan-shaped leaves of sugar maple, Canada's national symbol. Indigo fingers clawed into the mountainous forests at the coast, creating myriad inlets and bays, many accessible only by air and sea.

Howe Sound was the first major inlet past Vancouver, just a few minutes to the northwest. They descended over the tiny rustic community of Horseshoe Bay, across the southern tip of Bowen Island and the scattered islets to the north of Pasley. Finally the PB descended low across the southern peninsula of Keaton Island and came in for a landing in the Shoal Channel. The *Daedalus* followed as the aquatic biplane taxied to a small harbor area, pulling up into a ramshackle marina of timber wharfs.

Just up the hill from the docks, Jack could see what looked like a fortified camp from the Old West. A series of log-built barracks lined one end of an open parade ground, with a few larger timber and clapboard structures he reckoned were administrative offices, recreational facilities, and the like. The fort was enclosed by five-foot-high post-and-plank fencing, painted milk white, as if to say, "Keep out, but enjoy your day." A flagpole in front of what appeared to be the main structure flew the Red Ensign, a scarlet flag with a small version of the Union Jack emblazoned on the upper left, the Canadian coat of arms on the right.

As the shadow of the airship fell across the harbor, a collection of Squamish natives and white workers stood staring skyward, mouths agape. The initial shock was short-lived, however, and soon the docks were flooded with helping hands, cleating the XPB-1 to the first open slip. Aluminum cables plunged from the airship's gondola, and the rag-tag ground crew guided the *Daedalus* to a mooring tower of sorts. It had been assembled from raw timbers, much like a cone of telephone poles driven into the ground at angles to serve as an anchor. Jack assumed the RCMP had erected it specifically for their needs, as he wasn't sure how much airship traffic Gibsons Landing actually got in a given year.

Within a couple of minutes, the ship was winched nose-in to the tower, with the aft cargo ramp lowered to a long section of wharf. Four additional cables were secured to various nearby harbor pylons.

Although they'd never seen a dirigible up close, most everyone of the locals had been to the "flickers" and knew the exploits of the *Daedalus* crew as depicted in the adventure serials and newsreels. The existence of the AEGIS organization was no secret, but the occupants of the airship who stepped out onto the waterfront may as well have been movie stars for all of their mystery and allure.

Sparks and Deadeye took up positions near the cargo door as MacLennan hailed a cadre of dock workers and Mounties vying for a handshake with Captain Stratosphere.

An officer of medium height with a slicked crop of chestnut hair and a pencil mustache approached the wharf. He wore the customary high-collared red serge uniform jacket and navy jodhpur trousers of the Royal Canadian Mounted Police, a khaki flat-brimmed Stetson perched atop his head. "Captain McGraw, I assume?"

Jack turned to look, extending his right hand as the officer made his way forward through the small crowd. "That would be me," Jack smiled.

Doc almost gasped as the man took Jack's hand and shook it firmly. She thought he was a dead ringer for Douglas Fairbanks.

"Corporal Stevens," the man offered. "I handle the day-to-day here at the barracks. Sergeant-Major Banks is our commanding officer. Let me officially welcome our AEGIS friends to Gibsons Landing. I'm to bring you up to the office for an introduction and brief chat."

"Good to meet you, Corporal," said Jack. "This is our medical officer, Doctor Dorothy Starr."

Doc reached out and shook Stevens' hand, distracted enough by the handsome officer that she missed the brief swell of blue-white glow from the crystal lodestone hanging from her neck. It was gone as quickly as it had started. "Corporal," she nodded, smiling. Then, indicating Ellen, she added, "And this is our new officer-in-training, Junior Aeronaut Ellen Starr."

"Callsign Red." Ellen saluted, snapping her gum, which earned a smile and a salute in reply.

"She comes with us," Jack warned. "We're a package deal."

Initially surprised at the presence of a ten-year-old, Stevens grinned, and Doc could almost see the theatrical effect of sunlight glinting off his pearly teeth.

"Of course!" Stevens agreed. "We have special perks for Junior Aeronauts here!"

Ellen put her hands on her hips and squinted at him. "Like what?"

"Like a phonograph," Stevens answered without missing a beat. "And root beer...and if it won't scare you too much, we've got a stuffed grizzly in the canteen!"

Ellen pursed her lips as if negotiating, ultimately nodding in the affirmative. "Okay."

As Corporal Stevens turned to lead them away from the dock, Jack leaned over to Cipher and said softly, "Keep an eye on the ship. You've got command while we're away."

"Affirmative," Cipher replied, watching Stevens as he strode toward the complex of single-story timber buildings at the center of the village.

Jack, Doc, and Ellen followed the Mountie up the steps to a gravel street that ran in front of the Gibsons Landing general store, weaving past civilians and dock workers. Cipher watched them go, not noting the almost instantaneous flash of light between the RCMP bunkhouses and trading post. Nor the tiny, doll-like construct which peered around the side of a nearby rain barrel, taking in the aircraft and the gathered workers through its single golf-ball-sized eye.

- CHAPTER 10 -

The office was precisely what one would have expected from a Mountie headquarters. A box of stacked, hand-hewn logs with a potbelly stove in one corner, desk opposite the entry door. Curtained windows behind the desk overlooked the barracks assembly area. A modest gun cabinet held a collection of both small and large-caliber rifles, as well as a number of sidearms. A 1929 calendar was tacked to the wall to the left of the windows, a cork board to the right, covered in official memos and the occasional *WANTED* poster. A rack of antlers mounted to the right of the front door held a red uniform coat and tan Stetson. The sound of percolating coffee issued from the metal carafe on the flat top of the wood stove.

Sergeant-Major Banks leaned a flank on the edge of the desk, perusing a sheaf of papers with one hand, holding a tin coffee mug in the other, periodically sipping from it with delicate precision. He was a younger man—much younger than Jack had expected, especially given the apparent youth of Corporal Stevens. He was pale-complected, ginger and skinny, with round, wire-rim specs perched on a button nose. His white shirt sleeves were rolled to the elbow, revealing coils of muscle and a collection of impressive scars.

"Wolverine," Banks said, and Jack realized he and Doc had both been staring at the array of cicatrices along the man's left arm, from wrist to elbow.

Stevens shut the door behind them, announcing their presence. "Captain McGraw, Doctor Starr, and Junior Aeronaut Starr—"

"Callsign Red," Ellen whispered, nudging him in the ribs.

"Callsign Red," Stevens repeated.

Banks raised an eyebrow over the rim of his glasses and grinned. "Welcome, Red." He shifted from the desk and raised his mug in salute. "Welcome all. Coffee's hot. Help yourselves."

Jack still had questions. "Wolverine, huh?" As impressive as his own wounds would be, if cataloged and recited, carrying the scars from a wolverine attack nevertheless struck him as fascinating.

Banks chuckled, glancing over his scarred forearm as it held the steaming coffee. "Yeah, I was fourteen. Extended wilderness camp with the Scouts. I'd snared a rabbit and was cleaning it for supper, and the nasty thing decided the meal was his."

Doc was intrigued. "They must have incredibly sharp claws."

"Yes ma'am," Banks replied. "Sharp claws indeed. And teeth." He took a sip of coffee and winked at her. "But my knife was sharper."

Stevens smiled. "They had wolverine *and* rabbit stew!"

"Corporal," Banks ordered, his smile disappearing, "keep an eye on the aircraft at the harbor. I don't want any of the locals getting curious. There's heavy ordnance being moved, fer Pete's sake."

Stevens snapped to salute. "Sir!" he addressed, making his way to the door. On the way out, he collided with MacLennan coming in.

"Pardon me, sir," Stevens fumbled, dancing from side to side with MacLennan until the older man physically moved him out of the way.

"Dockside, Corporal," MacLennan uttered brusquely. "Supervise the ordnance transfer."

Stevens saluted again, despite nobody looking, or caring for that matter. "Sir!"

The door shut behind him, and MacLennan swept into the room. "Banks, is it?"

"Yessir," the Sergeant-Major nodded, saluting with his right hand while still holding the coffee with his left. "You MacLennan?"

"Inspector," came the almost irritated reply.

Banks turned his head to mask his eyes rolling back. "Of course, Inspector MacLennan."

"I was curious, Sergeant-Major Banks, why we were not greeted with more security at the docks."

Jack and Doc exchanged a silent look of surprise. Neither had heard MacLennan utter words that could be described as anything but civil. Perhaps now that he was back on his home turf, he felt at ease to display a less diplomatic side.

Banks raised his scarred forearm and took another sip of coffee. Jack was impressed at the man's poker face.

"Because most of my detachment is up at Panther Peak," Banks replied calmly. "Tracking the Sullivan gang." He rounded the back of the desk, gently setting the metal mug on a small quilted coaster. "Law enforcement of an immediate nature being our directive, and the weapons test being assigned after my men had left, this is what we have to work with."

MacLennan grew flushed. Jack could tell he was none too happy with the operation so far. "Very well," he said, finally. "We only have the resources we have. Fair enough. But for the duration of the testing, I want that corporal assigned night watch at the docks." He seemed to relax momentarily, then his shoulders bunched up and he added, "No one goes near either aircraft without specific orders and clearance."

"To be clear," Jack interjected, trying to lower the temperature somewhat, "we won't be in your hair for long. Couple days at most."

Doc put her hands on her hips. "And Ellen and I can see to our own amusement."

"Right," MacLennan nodded. "We'll need accommodations for these two ladies."

Banks sniffed and gave a disinterested shrug. "They can have their pick of the bunkhouses while my guys are away."

"Say," Jack offered, "could we help in any way regarding the Sullivan gang?"

MacLennan spun to look at Jack, incredulous.

"I mean when we're done with the test," Jack explained. "I expect maybe our little airship could be handy up on the mountain."

Banks gave a chuckle. "I do not disagree," he said. "We'll take a look when you're done and see where we are then. Thanks, Captain."

"Then we're set," MacLennan said formally, attempting to orchestrate a consensus. "First test run after lunch, when ordnance has been loaded. What's the status on targets?"

Banks shifted some papers and pointed out a few locations on a chart of the local area. "We've got six derelict trawlers anchored in the Strait of Georgia. Gliders will be towed from the airfield at Vancouver. Army gave us three of those."

Ellen padded to the window behind the desk and peered out at the vacant parade square.

"Captain?" MacLennan glanced at Jack. "What's your preference?"

Jack ran a meaty hand along his jaw and sighed. "Air-to-sea first," he reckoned. "It'll get us familiar with the system before we try air-to-air targeting."

"Sound reasoning," MacLennan offered. "I'll monitor radio communications here at base, but you're in command of the operation in the air."

The men nodded along, and Doc wormed her way in under Jack's left shoulder, wrapping an arm around his waist as they consulted the maps and charts on the desk. She still couldn't put her finger on why, but she felt in her bones that something was *off*.

Terribly, terribly *off*.

❧

Colonel Shaw watched the passenger biplane circle the airfield at Cricklewood, a late afternoon breeze teasing at his prematurely snowy hair. The airliner sported the black and red dual chevrons of Imperial Airways, coming in low and slow for a graceful landing.

Behind him stood the Handley Page factory and aerodrome, officially shuttered due to suburban development in the surrounding London boroughs. However the SIS—and by extension, the AEGIS London Bureau—still had access to the airfield and facilities until November. And that meant Shaw had a training center for his pet project.

In broad daylight, the man cut a distinguished and stereotypically British figure: lean and angular, well-groomed and fashionably dressed, the mystery of his missing eye hidden behind a wall of English reserve far stronger and more impervious than the eyepatch itself.

Flanking him was the Roma woman, Mila, in her worn military fatigues and long coat, hat and mantle. She clutched a heavily modified Henry rifle with a walnut stock, sniper scope, and a "brass knuckles" Winchester lever in place of the stock one.

On Shaw's other side stood a mechanical construct the approximate height and shape of a woman, an assemblage of chrome and brass finish, finely-crafted gears, and electronic wiring. Two discerning eyes glowed neon green from their sockets over a delicate nose and simple horizontal opening that served as a mouth. Ribbons of the same emerald light shone from the seams in joints and surface segments. Aluminum-plated boots both protected and stabilized the robotic legs within. The only other attempts at actual clothing were a utility belt with medical supply pouches strapped to the right thigh, and a short-cut pilot's jacket of the same brown leather as the belt, sleeves truncated and fastened at the elbows.

The android was known as Evelyn 4 among Shaw's top-secret circles, all because the lead roboticist had thought it would be a good idea to name the project after his late aunt. In July of 1918, Mary Harris, a battlefield nurse with the Queen Alexandra's Imperial Military Nursing Service at the Western Front, had been mortally wounded by a German shell. Shaw, already a rising star in the Secret Intelligence Service, had Mary's undamaged brain stem installed in a mechanical body as part of a pilot program to assist soldiers in the field with specialized automatons. Then the war ended that November, and the program was scrapped before it could be fully implemented.

Ultimately, the process had proved viable, if not exactly practical. Even so, Evelyn 4 was one of a kind.

Finally, a short, broad man in work clothes and a dun-colored bush hat treaded silently to Shaw's right. His face was a horror to behold: a patchwork of skin grafts, primitive reconstructive surgery, and the resulting scar tissue almost created the image of a living mannequin. Dark hazel eyes blinked through a tight skin mask of Asian ethnicity. Abhik Bhandari, decorated Gurkha commando now retired from the Royal Army, had been another of Shaw's special projects. One of countless veterans disfigured by explosive ordnance on the Western Front, the Nepalese soldier had been given access to the best psychological and medical care the Empire had to offer, and been allowed to continue his physical training for special covert operations. By Shaw's estimation, if left to his own devices, Bhandari would have eventually ended his own life. He'd seen it happen all too often, especially with those carrying the extra weight of battlefield disfigurement. It was inevitable: either through drink, or narcotics, or by his own hand. Instead, Shaw did what he could to repair some of the damage done to the man, to restore some dignity, to keep the hearth alight. After all, one didn't simply throw out a good gardening tool when it acquired a broken handle. One repaired the broken piece, had the blade sharpened, and got a few more years of use from it.

Bhandari was just too good at his job to put him out to pasture. And that was that.

Rule Britannia.

"Ah, good," Shaw sighed, squinting at the plane. "The French contingent."

The biplane taxied to a concrete strip near the terminal, rotary engines thundering to a stop as the reception committee gathered in front of the main hangar and two ground crewmen ran to secure and unbutton the aircraft. While the group watched, a man of African extraction, average height and athletic in build, exited the passenger cabin, U.S. Army duffel bag slung over his shoulder. He wore a gray twill suit and white fedora, and as he approached the group on the tarmac, they gradually became aware that his eyes were completely devoid of pigment.

Bhandari stared, intrigued. The man was ostensibly blind. He should not have been able to clear the two-hundred intervening feet without some form of assistance. A cane, perhaps.

A smile crept across Mila's face. She knew something.

"Joe Desmond," Shaw introduced with a wry smile. "Seer."

The new visitor reached out a hand, and Shaw shook it.

"Colonel Shaw," said Desmond, scanning the group with "sightless" eyes that, for some reason, took in far more information than mere visual data. "Good to see you again."

"Indeed," Shaw smiled. "I trust your flight was comfortable."

"Can't complain. Any word from Graves?"

Colonel Shaw shifted his weight. "Gunshade? He won't be joining us for this party. Working an operation in Chicago." He turned to the group and gestured. "Let me introduce you to your team members..." As Shaw made the other introductions, the ground crew wheeled a polished casket of black-lacquered pine from the plane's cargo hold to the assembled agents, where they parked the dolly, coffin and all. Without a word or odd look, the crewmen disappeared into the hangar, and all eyes but Desmond's went to the casket on wheels.

"Any trouble with Therese?" Shaw inquired, admiring the brass handles and inset cross on the lid.

Joe Desmond cocked his head and smiled. "Not at all," he said assuredly, caressing the casket's shiny finish with a calloused hand. "In fact, she's raring to go."

- CHAPTER 11 -

The growl of twenty diesel engines churned within a sea of clouds, and an immense gray silhouette gradually breached the billowy ceiling. The stern flight hangar broke through first, wisps of vapor trailing from the corners of the structure. Then the long, flat spine of the supercarrier appeared, with white landing stripes painted lengthwise.

As the massive mechanical leviathan ascended through the clouds, the topside landing strip gave way to a more bulbous undercarriage, its envelope resembling a torpedo squashed from above. Beneath the superstructure of perforated aluminum and vulcanized canvas skin, a command bridge was slung under the nose, meeting an extended gondola section that ran most of the length back.

Large segments of the ship's sides were occupied by gun ports—currently closed—where they weren't obscured by an engine spitting black smoke in their wake.

The airship bore the white four-pointed-star insignia of the *Astrum Argentum*, its name, *Osiris,* displayed aft in German lettering. There were no registry or model numbers on the tail assembly or sides; the *Osiris* had no home port and was one of a kind. Furthermore, as the Silver Star claimed no nationality, they felt no obligation to give any government a way to catalog the craft. She was simply *Osiris*, and if she appeared over your town or village, you'd be lucky if you survived to tell the tale.

The bridge was expansive, with two control stations, two radio consoles, and a large chart table set beneath a raised walkway from the entry door. The forward windscreen array was equally massive, with a 180-degree field of view left to right, and 90 degrees forward and down.

Maria Blutig stood on the upper gantry, leaning forward on the railing above the navigation table. Her uniform was clean and smartly pressed, ice-blue eyes staring from beneath the shiny black brim of her officer's cap.

Jonas Ecke stood next to the chart table on the main bridge floor, dressed in his smart black officer's uniform, arms clasped behind his back.

"Come three degrees south-southwest," he barked. "And stay on that heading."

"Three degrees south-southwest, aye!" answered each of the helmsmen, a Brit and a Swede, respectively. They wore flat airman caps and gray uniforms, each clutching a huge steering wheel.

Swaying in place at Maria's right shoulder, the pale, haunted form of Captain Hummel cast a sidelong glance toward her with two emerald points of light. He neither breathed nor spoke, simply standing on guard in his well-worn uniform and long coat. He smelled of low tide and death. If any part of his reanimated corpse was aware that he stood upon the bridge of his old ship, their mission now commanded by his chief rival within the Silver Star, he showed no sign. There was only the impulse to serve. The only goal: vengeance.

As if possessed of the same thought, Maria tilted her head to address Hummel quietly. "Not long, *Schwarzhund,*" she assured him. "Our reckoning is close at hand."

Then her eyes sought the table below her railing, and she opened her arms wide, parallel with it. "The Master speaks!"

Ecke snapped his attention to the center of the chart table as a dreamlike apparition flickered into being. He recognized the egg-shaped head of the grand magus himself, Aleister Crowley. It was not his first occasion to be present at an interdimensional address from the Master, but he'd never become used to the experience. He hoped he never would.

The shape swirled in psychotropic color, finally congealing into the familiar countenance every agent of the Silver Star knew and revered.

"The hour is nearly upon us," a nasally voice echoed from the ether. "The hour of the Red Storm, which will strike a blow for the *Astrum Argentum*, against the forces of AEGIS."

"Behold, Master," Maria addressed, standing at the fore of her assembled undead. "I have brought Captain Hummel—returned him, and the others, from icy twilight. I am prepared—"

"You will stay on the *Osiris*," Crowley interrupted, "to command the operation in the air."

Maria looked surprised for the first time in recent history, exchanging a glance with Ecke.

"But Master," she protested, "you said I would
—"

Crowley again interrupted. "I trust you do not question my judgment. In other circumstances, I would keep Ecke on the bridge, for he has superior combat experience in the air. However, for this mission, I require you to remain my conduit, to control the storm."

Maria stood silent, watching the disembodied head of her master as it droned on.

"Captain Ecke, you shall lead the ground assault. There are munitions being stored within the supply depot at Gibsons Landing. I want those missiles."

The bearded German sky captain stood agape. There was to be a ground assault, consisting of Maria's recently resurrected undead, he presumed. To steal the new AEGIS test weapons. And he was to lead this mixed force of once-dead Inuit, Norse, and Silver Star soldiers? Despite his confusion and creeping terror, he nodded in the affirmative. "*Jawohl*, Master."

"Acknowledged, my Master," Maria nodded, as the apparition began to warp and fade to transparency until it finally disappeared. She looked up, addressing the entire bridge crew. "Prepare for portal jump."

The two helmsmen exchanged a worried glance.

Had she just said *prepare for portal jump?*

As Maria stood majestically at the rail, her eyes rolled back white in her head, and her slender, talon-like fingers wrapped around the banister, as if claiming it as a conducting element. Hands erupted in a glow of unearthly green. Her jaw relaxed, mouth falling open as the sound of Hell itself burst forth from within her slender frame. The inner framework of the supercarrier began to shudder. A blinding flash seared through the bridge, followed by what could only be described as the sound of an exploding freight train crashing through a thunder cloud.

The helmsmen flinched. One of the radio women gasped in horror.

The massive airship bucked and pitched forward. The peaceful blue skies outside were instantly replaced by the swirling orange embers of a dark, ungodly abyss.

☙

Fifteen minutes later, Doc noticed that Ellen was no longer in the office with them. Leaving Jack to complete the planning for the afternoon's weapon test, she slipped out through the door and followed her daughter's most likely trajectory down to the water.

She found the ten-year-old perched atop a split-rail fence above the harbor, watching as dock workers unloaded various non-essential gear from the *Daedalus* cargo hold.

Their duffel bags and two of the three JP10 jet packs from the cargo bay sat piled nearby, along with the Dugdale, a lightweight experimental electric motorcycle known for having the most uncomfortable sidecar in history.

Eventually Jack emerged from the command office with MacLennan and Banks in tow. Banks ordered the pile of gear on the wharf to be transported and stowed at the fort, and it slowly worked its way off the dock in pieces, under local muscle.

Jack and Doc shared a brief but passionate kiss, and Ellen leaped into her father's embrace. Setting her back on the fence, he ruffled her hair and smiled.

"You ladies take care of one another. We'll be back for supper."

Doc wasn't used to feeling left out of the action like this, but she kept repeating to herself, *It's only a weapon test. Only a weapon test. Not your wheelhouse.*

As Jack joined Deadeye, Cipher, and Sparks aboard the *Daedalus*, Ellen tugged at her mother's shirt. The exterior doors and hatches were secured from inside, and a breeze kicked up from the airship turbofans.

"Hey Mom, why does Corporal Stevens get to go on the test?"

Doc puzzled, lines forming on her brow. "What do you mean, honey? He's *not* going."

Ellen scratched her head, smoothing out her hair where her father had messed it. "I saw him go aboard when they were loading the rockets. He never came out."

Doc felt a familiar tingle at the base of her skull, a signal she'd learned to trust over time. But then she glanced toward the RCMP office and noticed Corporal Stevens directing a dock worker toward one of the bunkhouses, and pointed for Ellen's benefit. "No, see, honey? There he is, up there, at the top of the path."

Ellen followed her mother's gesture and took in the sight of Corporal Stevens. She could have sworn she never saw him exit the airship.

"Come on, honey," Doc instructed. "We're in the barracks by Sergeant-Major Banks' office."

Frustrated and perplexed, Ellen cast a worried glance upward as the *Daedalus* rose into the afternoon sky, her father at the helm.

❦

"By the strength of my Will, let this circle obey its nature, and likewise the eldritch powers beyond our mortal realm obey my command."

Aleister Crowley raised his arms, the loose sleeves of ceremonial robes falling back to his elbows. His forearms were bloodstained, the palms upturned. He stood in the same conservatory, the floor now adorned in a complex array of symbols scrawled in white chalk. The image of a long snake coiled around the center of the great Circle of Solomon, while a smaller triangle pointed west, opposite its usual easterly orientation. A selection of smaller arcane shapes radiated outward, bathed in the flickering glow of large candles.

His nameless servant trembled slightly in the dim light of the room; he'd witnessed far more today than he'd ever bargained for. And it was far from over.

The Master chanted the invocation for the portal opening as he had done hours previously, a slowly whirling rift in space and time stretching from nothingness into a shimmering, mirror-like image: the bridge of the *Osiris* suddenly blinked into view, engines roaring as a red-orange hellscape passed under the windscreens. Tendrils of ethereal smoke and spouts of flame erupted beneath the ship, and Crowley knew it was taking every ounce of Maria's will to keep the massive zeppelin steady on course. One pinpoint leak in a single ballonet is all it would take for a sulfurous jet of flame to ignite the hydrogen keeping the ship aloft. He wasn't sure which dimension they now traversed together; he wondered if it was the same one Maria had called home for a year. It would make the most sense, as she would have knowledge of navigating the place.

Almost instantly, there was a blinding flash from the portal, and the *Osiris* bridge was now backlit by a deep blue sky and the orb of a bright summer sun. The crew staggered as a single entity. One of the helmsmen leaned over and vomited onto the perforated aluminum floor.

The Master was impressed. Maria had ushered a massive, hydrogen-filled airship through not one, but two-dimensional rifts. They had passed through one of many hells and arrived safely back in the material plane. In doing so, they had cut their usual travel time by nearly a week. Even in the most powerful of the arcane secret societies outside the *Astrum Argentum*, this was simply unheard of.

And that didn't even take into account the *secondary* portal he had opened into the *Osiris* while in transit. They were truly ascendant in their power now.

"Captain Ecke," Crowley addressed. "You may lead your ground assault."

The white-bearded airship captain gazed back through the portal, into the conservatory in England, into the dark eyes of The Great Beast of Mankind. He dared not linger.

"*Jawohl,*" Ecke saluted, turning on his heel to leave the bridge.

The group of undead soldiers Maria had resurrected from the Arctic shipwreck followed silently out of Crowley's field of view.

"Are you ready, my child?" Crowley purred. Despite the soft tone, his words reverberated through the portal and onto the *Osiris* bridge. His view was from behind Maria as she stood aft of the chart table, looking past the helmsmen into the deep blue sky outside the carrier's windows. As he watched, Maria bowed her head, whether out of deference or exhaustion he couldn't be sure. But then she raised it again, rolling her shoulders back, as she prepared to become a conduit for Crowley's mystical power—not merely a conduit, a combustion chamber, fed by his power and her own.

The corners of Aleister Crowley's lips turned up, and he contorted his hands into a series of arcane gestures, feeling the invoked energies of ancient, unearthly beings well within his psyche. Feeling the plentiful reservoir of life force given him by his followers. "Then let us begin," he instructed. "Let us summon the storm."

- CHAPTER 12 -

The *Daedalus* soared above Gibsons Landing. Turbofans sang their beehive song as Jack pulled back on the flight yoke and applied forward throttle. He saluted out the large bank of windscreens encircling the front half of the bridge, watching as Doc and Ellen waved from the wharf below. In minutes, they'd be buttoned up safely inside the RCMP fort.

The plan was simple: the *Daedalus* would head west into the Strait of Georgia. There they would find their first target, try out the radio targeting lock and firing mechanism, then move on to the next derelict boat, and repeat.

"All stations," Jack addressed in a clear tone, "report in."

Cipher was the first to respond, sitting just behind and to his left. "Comms ready and standing by, sir."

From the engine room, Sparks' young Kenyan accent crackled into Jack's earpiece. "Engines ready, output nominal, standing by."

"Uh, weapon system...ready, I guess?" Deadeye's monotone status report arrived from the forward turret below. "Payload is six...torpedoes. I dunno, what are we calling these things?"

"Don't worry, Charlie," Jack smiled, working a piece of his licorice chewing gum as he spoke into the headset mic. "'Torpedo' is fine. Command will get the lingo locked down, but that's above our pay grade."

Cipher squinted at the curved green screen on the radio detector console and finessed the tuning dial. The now-familiar *deet-deet-deet* of the signal emitter had become mere background noise to the crew over time.

"Captain," she hailed, touching her left hand to her headset, "I have a nautical vessel at anchor approximately two miles dead ahead, if you stay on your present heading."

"Got it," Jack announced. "I'm gonna keep her at a thousand feet, fifty miles per hour on approach." Adjusting the throttle with his left hand, he added, "Let me know when you have radio lock."

Below them, the shadow of the *Daedalus* rippled along the water's surface like the dark silhouette of a massive orca. In the distance, the gray form of an old fishing trawler bobbed in the water, devoid of crew. It was streaked with rust and eaten full of holes above the waterline, and Jack noted the complete absence of human activity in the vicinity.

Amber warning lights flashed from the guidance system where the navigation desk once stood.

Cipher flipped a toggle switch on the radio console. "Target has radio lock, Captain."

"Okay, Charlie," Jack warned into the headset. "Fire when ready."

Deadeye's baritone crackled into Jack's ear. "Firing."

As Cipher and Jack watched from the cockpit, a rocket projectile about two feet long ejected forward from beneath them and shot away into the distance. A trail of gray smoke sat in its wake. Lights flashed on the radio guidance machine in the nav station, and a series of accelerating electronic beeps told the crew the missile was approaching its intended target.

A plume of fiery debris showed them the weapon had worked as intended. The trawler erupted in a display of rocketing embers and flying chunks of rusty metal, which hissed and fizzled as they plunged into the cold waters of the strait.

Cipher gave her instrumentation panel a quick scan. "Direct hit, Captain."

"Good work, crew," Jack noted. "*Daedalus* to Base—primary target destroyed. Proceeding to secondary target."

MacLennan's voice interjected over the comms. "Base to *Daedalus*—affirmative."

As with the first, Cipher located the derelict fishing boat at anchor about two miles north, and Jack made a low and slow approach. This time, however, he would test the limits of the guidance system by having Deadeye fire the rocket at the outer range as written in the technical specs.

Had to keep his crew on their toes, even on a fairly by-the-numbers exercise.

"Lock target as soon as you can, Cipher."

Amber warning lights flashed again.

"Target locked, Captain."

Jack had honed an already-impressive spatial awareness to uncanny levels during his time in the Royal Flying Corps during the

Great War, and he knew they were just outside the one-mile maximum range given in the Boeing specs. "Alright, Charlie. Fire when ready."

Expecting a response and receiving none, Jack hit his *TALK* button again. "Charlie? Fire rocket two."

A full second passed. Then three.

"Charlie?"

Another five seconds expired, the only answer static. The airship rattled briefly as a gust of wind hammered the outer envelope.

Cipher's radio detector console suddenly lit up with warning lights, but her attention was drawn to the bridge door

Jack scowled. "What's your status, Deadeye?"

"Captain?" Cipher asked meekly, and Jack turned in the pilot's chair to respond.

Deadeye stood in the bridge doorway, aiming a black Army Colt .45 at his friends.

ॐ

"To the insertion point!"

Captain Jonas Ecke strode to the open landing platform that made up the top spine of the *Osiris*. The wind played at his officer's cap and threatened to knock it from his head, but Ecke always wore his head cover tight for just these occasions.

Stepping into the aluminum gyro-skiff, boat-shaped with twin rotors, he noted it was helmed by a living Silver Star airman, a fellow German by the look of him. Aside from the man, the rest of the landing party was made up of what Greenlanders and Norse folk called *draug*. The reanimated dead, resplendent in shredded clothing and dripping viscera, with glowing green pinpoint eyes. The bodies of 19th century Norwegian sailors, native Inuits, one Viking throwback, and a small handful of Silver Star commandos, not the least of which was Captain Ernst Hummel, the *Schwarzhund* of the *Astrum Argentum*, former commander of the *Osiris*.

The mission parameters were clear: make landing in the forest just outside the RCMP compound at Gibsons Landing, meet the Silver Star contact at the main gate. The fort should be devoid of most personnel. Go to the armory, secure the guided rocket ordnance being stored there. If possible, secure the capture—or death—of any AEGIS personnel encountered.

Ecke felt the weight of the MP-18 in his left arm and scowled beneath his frosty white sea captain's beard. He wasn't used to leading ground operations, but what with his own ship undergoing refit at their base in Samarkand, and the Master growing ever more maniacal as he was powerful, Ecke was unwilling to press the matter. If ground operations were what he was given, ground operations would have to do.

From what he'd been told, his unit of undead soldiers had been instructed with the parameters of the mission, and would follow his orders, so long as said orders didn't jeopardize said mission. He didn't like the sound of it. This had all the hallmarks of one of those "Everyone is expendable" operations Crowley was so fond of. Just throw everything at an impossible situation and see who survives. Especially now that he saw that he was to be the only living officer on the assignment.

And yet, if their intelligence was right, that their contact within the RCMP had actually emptied the fort and was ready to lead them in, it was entirely possible there existed a method to the madness.

This mission could actually work.

After being on the defensive for the past four years, essentially since AEGIS had engaged the crew of the *Daedalus*, the Silver Star hadn't exactly been getting a lot of wins, and what few there were had been hard-fought.

Ecke reached into his right front trousers pocket, fishing for a small jade stone he'd been keeping for almost a whole year, ever since his face-to-face encounter with Jack Mc-Graw and Dorothy Starr in the sky above Sanctuary Island. Running a calloused finger across its glossy surface reassured him as much as the presence of the symbol etched in its face. As he stepped aboard, he felt the skiff rise with the pitch of the rotors. Blinking against the ever-increasing winds, he gripped the submachine gun with both hands and shuddered.

The skiff descended over the Strait of Georgia, plunging through the lush, green canopy to a clearing just a few hundred meters outside the tiny trading post of Gibsons Landing.

Yes, he thought, stepping out onto the soft ground as the rotors and storm winds whipped discarded pine needles into a small tornado. *If I handle this mission with expert care, perhaps something will come of it.*

Captain Ecke braced himself against the wind and nodded toward the trail ahead. Twenty-three undead abominations followed silently.

Jack struggled with his harness. "Charlie? What the hell—?"

The Colt barked once. The bullet penetrated the pilot's chair and missed Jack's ribcage by mere inches. A blast of wind erupted from the center windscreen as it cracked into a spiderweb and the projectile rocketed out into the sky beyond.

Cipher was unstrapped in an instant, whirling out of her seat to snap a booted kick to Charlie's gun hand. The pistol flew wide, clattering across the former navigation console to the grated floor.

Jack hauled back hard on the stick and throttled full speed forward, just as a savage gust of wind slashed at the *Daedalus*, forcing the ship to nose up at a precarious angle. The sudden shift caused Deadeye to stumble backward, out the doorway and into the bowels of the ship.

Throttling down and leveling off the climb, Jack flipped a few of the engine toggles into a station-keeping configuration. With the smaller engines powered down, the ship could automatically use the large outboard thrusters to maintain a relatively stationary position and altitude for an indefinite period of time. He shrugged out of the pilot harness and followed Cipher toward the stairs. Across the main saloon, both could see a small, doll-like shape scamper toward the aft corridor and the engine room.

"What was that—?" Cipher gasped, as Jack leaped down the perforated stairwell to the main gantry and the access hatch to the forward weapon turret.

The hatch lay open, Charlie's unconscious body sprawled halfway out.

Jack knelt over his unconscious comrade, checking for injuries. His close-cropped raven hair was matted wet in back with blood which seeped onto the aluminum deckplate. Some-one—or some *thing*—had beaned him pretty hard. "Damn it," Jack muttered under his breath. "Come on, Charlie. I need you back, buddy."

A broadside of storm winds beat at the envelope, tossing the small airship like a football.

Jack found himself stymied for one of the few times in his life. If he left Deadeye in order to pilot the ship, his friend might die. If he allowed the weather system outside to batter the *Daedalus* at will, they *all* might die. And there was the matter of the strange critter running around the ship, wreaking havoc.

Order of operations, he thought, recalling his officer's training from the war. *Stabilize the ship.*

"Cipher, get to the bridge," he ordered, "See if you can get us above the storm."

Striding to the small galley, Jack pulled a thick cotton towel from a linen pantry, rolling it into a cylindrical shape as he knelt back down by Deadeye's unconscious form. He gently raised the sharpshooter's head, sliding the makeshift pillow beneath his neck.

"There you go, buddy."

Another gust of wind hit the envelope, and Deadeye jostled awake, rolling his eyes in agony. "Argh. Sonnovabitch got the drop on me."

Jack patted his chest. "It's okay, Charlie. You're gonna be okay."

The floor heaved and fell as the airship was hammered by the winds outside. Jack heard the outboard thrust engines straining at the inconstant air and leaped back up the stairs to the bridge. "Stay there, buddy! I'll be right back!"

Cipher was fighting the control yoke when Jack appeared behind her. One moment the ship was nose-up in the wind, the next it was diving toward the frigid waters below. It was nearly impossible to find up or down, and no horizon was visible through the cracked, rain-splattered windscreen.

Jack approached the pilot's chair from behind, grabbing the headrest for stability as he tried to scan the instrument panel. The liquid compass showed that the ship was being spun and thrown backward in a generally southerly heading.

"She's not responding," Cipher complained. "I can't get out of the storm."

Jack saw Cipher's grip tighten on the flight controls, and knew she was only a few moments from full-blown panic. He tried to offer some gentle coaching.

"It's okay, Cipher. Ease up. Don't fight her." Reaching across the control panel, he flipped the toggle switches to purge all ballast, releasing streams of water from tanks in the lower gondola. "This should gain us some altitude."

They both felt the ship begin to rise higher, and Cipher nodded, taking a deep breath.

"It's working," she said.

Jack cracked a brief smile. "Now just keep a loose hand on the stick and use the wind to push her."

A shout erupted from the engine room, followed by a crash, and more shouting.

The *Daedalus* vibrated with strong winds, and Jack heard the whine of the thrust engines die as the turbofans spun down.

He could feel it—they were drifting.

"Awww, don't tell me..."

Cipher pushed the throttle all the way forward and back several times, looking over the power gauges on the control panel. There was nothing to do.

"I've lost both outboard thrusters," she announced. "We're dead in the air."

- CHAPTER 13 -

While Sergeant-Major Banks and Inspector MacLennan availed themselves of the short--wave console in the radio shack, Doc and Ellen sat across from each other in a small timber-frame canteen, playing chess on a handcrafted board, sipping root beer from identical brown glass bottles.

It was odd having the run of the RCMP compound when it was as devoid of human life as it now was, with most of the Mounties away on the hunt for a criminal gang. The accommodations were plenty comfortable, if a bit rustic, but Doc was used to "roughing it", judging by her 7-by-10 stateroom on the *Daedalus*.

A low cloud rolled in off the Strait of Georgia, casting a wide shadow across most of Gibsons Landing. It quickly peeled away again, carried by a northwesterly breeze that slapped at the outside of the canteen.

"You can't do that," Ellen scolded with a bored look.

Doc blinked. *Do what?* She'd clearly not been paying attention.

"Your queen," Ellen explained.

Finally Doc saw it. By shifting her queen, she'd opened her king to check by Ellen's bishop. An illegal move. "Oh, sorry," she said, moving the queen back into the bishop's line of fire. She was tempted to take that pesky bishop with her queen, but Ellen had a knack for having a three-layered ambush laying in wait for such brash maneuvers. She looked for another piece to throw into the diagonal way of the ravenous bishop.

"What was that?" Ellen pondered, her attention suddenly drawn skyward through the window.

"What was what?" Doc answered with her own question, following her daughter's sight line. Before Ellen could answer, however, a crack of thunder echoed across the sky.

The wind picked up both velocity and muscle, rushing into the tiny coastal community and pummeling the small timber buildings in the compound. The sun seemed to fade on a dimmer to half-strength behind a thick cloud layer that barreled in from the north. A fat, stinging rain pelted down without mercy, forcing the dock workers and other Gibsons residents to find shelter indoors.

Just like that, the storm was on them. A storm whose swirling clouds had a distinctly crimson tinge.

"This doesn't look good," Doc worried, standing from the chair and making her way briskly to the door. "Come on, Ellen. Let's get to the radio shack and find out how your father is."

Ellen nodded in agreement, making a mental note of the placement of the chess pieces, should they return to their game at any point in the future. "Do you think they'll stop the test?"

"They'll have to, honey," Doc sighed. She really didn't like the looks of this weather system, or how quickly it had appeared. "The winds are too high for them to keep flying. If anything, they'll have to fly somewhere beyond the system, maybe get above it, and wait it out."

Ellen didn't answer. In her brief decade of life, there'd never been a time when one or both parents weren't in some kind of danger. As it was the normal state of affairs, she'd never learned to worry. Their profession was peril. They knew how to handle themselves. Her dad would be okay, or so she assumed.

But then she noticed the blue-white glow from the lodestone around her mother's neck, and a creeping sense of doubt—and dread—began to coil in the back of her mind.

Doc pulled her coat over the lodestone, not noticing. Ellen started to say something, but Doc had already opened the door.

Bracing against the blast of wind and rain, Doc and Ellen clutched their jacket collars tightly to their throats and forced their way out of the canteen. Green maple leaves, torn from their branches too early by the wind, leaped and circled in a widespread and chaotic ballet. The rain didn't so much as *fall* as it was shot from the barrel of a weather cannon. It stung their eyes and faces, making it nearly impossible to navigate the open parade square. They staggered at first, but Doc knew where the radio building was, and could just make out the glow of a kerosene lamp beckoning from a lone window.

It was perhaps the hardest forty meters either one of them had ever walked, but at long last, they arrived at the door to the radio shack. A polite knock was out of the question; Doc pounded a fist against the pine planks that made up the new door.

In seconds, Corporal Stevens filled the bright rectangle of the doorway. Inside the radio office, MacLennan and Banks were shouting: MacLennan into the radio, Banks ordering the Corporal to go stand guard over the rocket munitions in the armory.

"Ladies," Stevens saluted with a large flashlight, edging past the women and heading into the blustery gloom outside.

Doc and Ellen entered the small cabin, which was the spitting image of Banks' office. The only discernible difference was that the main desk, instead of supporting a leather blotter and the Sergeant-Major's flank, served as the platform for a large two-way wireless radio console. Doc pushed the door shut with a *thud*.

"Base to *Daedalus*! Please respond!" MacLennan bellowed into the handset microphone. The listening headset was cocked at an angle on his bald head, leaving his left ear uncovered.

Doc gave Banks a worried glance. "What's wrong?" she quietly demanded.

"We lost the *Daedalus* on the radio the moment the storm blew in."

Doc sighed. "Do you get these a lot up here?"

As she released her grip on her coat collar, the subtle, high-pitched ringing and pale blue glow from the lodestone filled the small office, grabbing the attention of the two men. Puzzled at first by their reaction, Doc finally glanced down and realized that her magic "barometer" was working.

"Um, no," Banks answered with a raised eyebrow. "You?"

Doc flushed, but quickly recovered, fingering the edge of the stone shard. "Fair question. This lodestone senses magical energies at work, and the fact that it's glowing pretty solidly right now tells me the storm isn't of a natural origin."

MacLennan glanced at the billowing red storm clouds outside the window and frowned. "No kidding?"

Ellen strode to the window and silently followed the silhouette of Corporal Stevens as he moved among the bunkhouses in the distance, the beam of his flashlight her only real point of reference. She gently tugged at her mother's coat, pointing out through the blustery weather at the bobbing light.

Doc squinted through the spatters and rivulets on the windowpane. "Sergeant-Major, where is the armory?"

Banks turned his attention from MacLennan and the radio console, moving closer to Doc at the window. He was back in his crimson uniform jacket, looking much more formal than when they'd met in his office. "Just on the far side of the canteen," he said. "Why?"

Doc pointed at the distant beam of light. It was heading toward the compound's main gate. "Then what's he doing at the gate?" she wondered aloud.

Banks frowned. "That's a damn good question."

Ellen shifted a quick glance at her mother, eyes wide as she noticed the lodestone growing steadily brighter.

"When you said your detachment was up the mountain, going after the Sullivan gang..." Doc turned to face Banks, pressing the point. "*Who* gave you that intelligence?"

Locking eyes with her, Banks went a shade paler than his ordinary ghostly complexion. "Corporal Stevens gave it to me in an official report," he said softly.

"Gentlemen," Doc addressed, returning her attention to the scene outside the window, "I believe you have a Silver Star agent in your ranks."

Banks and MacLennan watched with Doc and Ellen, as Corporal Stevens unbarred the main gate, swinging it wide to allow the gathered force to enter. Out of the blustery darkness came a collection of shambling silhouettes with glowing embers of emerald green where their eyes should have been.

- CHAPTER 14 -

"Try to hold her steady with the primaries!" Jack shouted from the bridge door. "I'll get back to the engine room, see what's what!"

As he pushed away from the hatch frame, an explosion thundered outside and the *Daedalus* suddenly pitched backward, tossing him ribs-first into the stairway handrail. He grunted with the impact, cursing under his breath. Living and working alongside Doc had exposed him to a repertoire of salty language he'd barely encountered in the air during the Great War. In recent years, he'd begun to employ more of it.

"What the hell was that?" he demanded, stepping back onto the bridge.

Cipher pointed out the cracked wind-screen. The sky was blood red and crackled with lightning. "It's an electrical storm, Captain," she explained. "But that felt more like a concussive impact—an explosive of some kind!"

He had to agree. They'd flown through electrical storms in the past. Not only could the *Daedalus* withstand a lightning strike, she was rigged with special wiring and circuits that charged the battery array while preventing overloads.

Jack's eyes grew wide as he realized what she was saying. "You mean...?"

Cipher turned as best she could to make eye contact as she fought to hold the ship steady with the four smaller engines placed fore and aft on either side of the envelope. "Yes sir," she breathed. "Someone's shooting at us."

Jack blinked. This was not happening. It couldn't be.

He knew the supercarriers employed by the Silver Star were four times the size of the *Daedalus*, even more prone to storm winds and foul weather than she was. Then there was the matter of how they'd managed to find the *Daedalus* in the middle of nowhere, British Columbia. Fortunately, on the one occasion they happened to have a captured LR3 AEGIS airship two years ago, the Silver Star put all their focus into the *Percival*'s electric dynamo generators and didn't bother to reverse-engineer the cockpit radio detector, if they'd even recognized it for what it was.

Another explosion rocked the outer hull, and Jack knew Cipher was right. It wasn't a lightning strike. It was a projectile exploding. It reminded him of anti-aircraft ground fire during the war, when he and his pilots would have to dodge blooms of flak on their way to an objective. He also knew that both the *Luftpanzer II* and the *Osiris* had a bank of anti-aircraft guns on each side of the respective ships.

He wasn't sure how they found him. He wasn't sure how such a leviathan could stay aloft in the middle of the same storm. But they were here, and they were shooting. At least without a radio detector, they were firing blind. Thank heaven for small mercies.

Jack made a move toward the radio console, and Cipher shook her head. "No good. The circuits for the radio and the radio detector are down."

"So it's not the storm interference?"

"No sir. The circuits are dead. Power likely cut from engineering."

Jack clenched his teeth, running the backs of his knuckles over his jaw, which was already starting to sprout some bristle. "Do what you can to keep us stable and out of range. Hidden if possible. Stay in the dense clouds."

"Aye, sir." Cipher flashed a petrified look and turned back to the helm controls.

Jack turned to retreat down the short stairwell to the main saloon, and found Dead-eye sitting almost upright, holding the towel to the back of his skull like a pillow.

"Anyone get the number of that truck?" he groaned.

Jack knelt by his old friend. "How you doing, buddy?"

"About as good as you look," came the sarcastic reply.

At least his sense of humor was intact. That was a good sign. Doing a quick optical check, Jack saw that Charlie's pupils were dilated and asymmetrical. "Boy howdy, you sure got your bell rung."

"Really?" Charlie muttered with mock incredulity. "Didn't notice."

Another explosion rumbled from outside, though it seemed to be far enough away that it could have been thunder.

"Don't wanna alarm you, Cap," Deadeye smirked, "but someone's shootin' at us."

"Yeah, I know. We're adrift in a storm I don't think was naturally-caused. Engines are down. We're sitting ducks."

"Maria?"

"That's my guess."

"I'm starting to think," Deadeye chuckled, but it came out as a cough, "she really doesn't like us."

A crash echoed through the main saloon, followed by shouting, and another crash. The cabin lights suddenly went dark, and the saloon was flooded with a familiar red emergency glow.

Jack shot a look toward the engine room. "I have to go check that out," he said. "You stay put and get your sea legs. Back me up when you can."

Deadeye nodded. "Go get 'em, Cap'n."

Jack sprinted aft, shucking one of his nickel-plated Colts as he ran. Lights flickered, and the exterior hum of engine fans spinning up and shutting down lit a fire of intention under him. A gust of storm wind slammed the ship from the port side, knocking him off-balance. He shifted his weight and recovered, nosing into the engine room.

Stepping over the hatchway threshold, he was met by a brutal right cross. His vision flashed white, then went momentarily dim as he fell against the main engineering console. Someone large had his gun hand pinned and was grabbing at his shoulder holster. The assailant pulled away, and Jack opened his eyes to look up into his spitting image, minus the swelling jaw and trickle of blood from the corner of his own mouth.

The attacker leveled the twin to his own automatic, a sly grin creeping across his face.

A tiny flaming shower erupted from the wall of gauges to his right, drawing Jack's attention down to the floor, where Sparks lay unconscious, socket wrench by her head.

He glanced back at the chiseled jaw and piercing blue eyes of his doppelganger and sighed. The impostor was identical to Jack in every way, from the day's growth of dark copper beard to the gray jacket and blue uniform trousers, to the leather flight cap and shoulder holster, which appeared to be full.

Whatever this thing was, it could mimic the look of something, but couldn't conjure an actual object. Hence the stolen Colt, now pointed at his chest.

"Well, shit."

❧

Doc found herself counting paces to the bunkhouse nearest the administration office, where she and Ellen had stowed their packs. One of which held something Doc very much wanted in her possession.

The swaying, shambling mass of glowing eyes was now pushing through the main gate into the open parade square.

"Gentlemen," she addressed Banks and MacLennan in her most serious tone, "unless I'm seriously off-base, and I don't think I am, we are about to be overrun by what the Nordic people call *draugr*. We don't have a lot of time for me to explain, but these are reanimated dead, infused with supernatural strength." She glanced down at Ellen and sighed. She'd hoped to be able to shield her daughter from this horror. But as she watched the emerald pinpoints of light bobbing in the distance, she knew all bets were off. Ellen was about to grow up a lot in the next several minutes. Turning back to the men, she added with authority, "They will tear you apart as you stand, and only complete immolation appears to slow them down."

Ellen shivered. She'd heard her parents discuss some details of their previous mission to the Arctic, in hushed tones after they thought she was in bed asleep.

Banks raised an eyebrow, perplexed. "Sorry, Doctor, did you say *'reanimated dead'*?"

"She did," MacLennan replied, and Banks saw him produce a Colt 1908 Pocket Hammerless pistol from inside his coat.

"And you're on board with that?" Banks asked him.

MacLennan sighed. "Sergeant-Major, one of our many charges at A Division is monitoring global threats. Trust me when I tell you the Silver Star is one of them."

The young Mountie officer blinked once, started to speak, then blinked again. He finally assembled the right words in his head. "So...all those movie serials, with Gary Cooper and Myrna Loy..."

Doc pursed her lips in frustration. She didn't have time for this. "Those are movies," she answered, adding, "but some of them are based on our actual missions." She shifted her focus to MacLennan, who was clearly more prepared to act. "Mr. MacLennan, I need to get to our bunkhouse. I'll need some cover." She reached toward her collar and pulled the softly glowing lodestone from around her neck, placing the silver chain over Ellen's head. The artifact hung lower on the ten-year-old's chest but continued its cool blue-white illumination unabated. "You need to keep the stone, honey," she instructed. "Keep it safe."

Ellen Starr, ever the self-reliant, rough-and-tumble girl, felt scared for the first time that day. Her eyes instantly became wet with tears, and her chin wobbled slightly as she looked up at Doc.

Doc immediately understood the implication and squatted down, sweeping Ellen into her arms. "Oh honey, no. No, I'm not leaving you." She gripped her daughter firmly by the shoulders and smiled, her own eyes welling up. "We're not splitting up."

Ellen instantly relaxed.

Doc stood, facing Banks and MacLennan. "Our best hope is to stick together. Don't split up. We get to the bunkhouse first, then the supply depot, or wherever you keep the kerosene."

Banks pulled his service revolver from its uniform holster, spinning the cylinder and checking to make sure it was fully loaded. "I have a can back at the office," he noted. "But if you need a lot, supply is probably best."

Doc glanced out the window, watching as the mob of glowing green eyes moved into the parade ground and split into small groups. "We're gonna need a lot."

MacLennan frowned, doing some basic math. "We've got, what, thirteen rounds between the two of us," he reckoned, indicating Banks' revolver and his own automatic. "We're going to need some more firepower if we really hope to make a dent in those...*drog...drag...*"

"*Draugr*," Doc corrected.

"Got some rifles back at the office," Banks noted. "But there's more at the armory."

"And the armory is where the new rockets are being stored," MacLennan added. "Doctor, is there any chance these things are here to steal the munitions?"

Doc shrugged. "Sometimes with the Silver Star, it's a random attack, to probe our strength. But sometimes..." She trailed off, thinking about what a perfect opportunity this was for a Silver Star operation: a legendary AEGIS ship in the air with a skeleton crew, with their chief medical officer on the ground at an all-but-deserted RCMP fort. If Corporal Stevens was indeed an agent of the *Astrum Argentum*, he would have been able to communicate plans and strategies and orchestrate a means of getting rid of the Mounties at the fort. Doc swallowed. "Sometimes they know exactly how to hit us for maximum impact."

Banks shook his head in the affirmative. "We should assume that's what they're here for."

"We need to secure the rockets," MacLennan agreed.

Doc stepped away from the window, corralling Ellen toward the slatted door.

All four of the cabin's occupants could hear the storm whistle outside.

"Bunkhouse first," she instructed, plucking an iron fire poker from next to the wood stove in the corner. "There's something there that can help us. Then we hit the armory. That can be our Alamo if need be." She looked at Banks, who nodded back. Turning to MacLennan, she found his gaze through a pair of slightly fogged spectacles. He saw her nonetheless and nodded as well.

Doc crouched and touched her forehead to Ellen's. "You stay right next to me, no matter what happens." Taking a moment to tuck the lodestone hanging from Ellen's neck into her shirt collar, she smiled. "Make your father proud."

Ellen saluted. "Affirmative." It was astonishing how little fear she had when she and her mother were together.

Sergeant-Major Banks put his shoulder to the door and cracked it open to the night. The storm blew leaves and debris, scattering it in all directions, wet with spattered rain. The afternoon was dark as night. No sign of the glowing eyes pierced the haze. No voices could be heard above the howling winds. With the revolver in his right hand, door braced open with his left, Banks stepped into the maelstrom.

Doc clutched Ellen to her left side, brandishing the fire poker in her right.

MacLennan took up the rear guard, gripping the pocket automatic in a left hand that should not have been sweating so much, given the low temperature outside. "Let's go," he grunted.

They ran into the wind and stinging rain, red clouds roiling above.

- CHAPTER 15 -

"Who...what are you?" Jack demanded, but the duplicate only stood there with a sinister grin and the stolen pistol held at the ready. "Damnit," Jack cursed. "You're not gonna wreck my ship!"

"You're not gonna wreck my ship," the thing repeated, in Jack's own baritone. The corners of the doppelganger's lips turned up even more cartoonishly, and Jack knew whatever this was had interpreted his threat as a direct challenge. He knew there was a bullet with his name on it in the duplicate's gun, and he expected it to enter his body at any second.

The wind outside was interrupted by a thundering explosion, buckling the airship's envelope and sending it spiraling like a top at the end of a spin. Jack suddenly came face to face with the duplicate as both pistols fired.

Jack felt his left bicep give way to the force of the doppelganger's bullet as he kicked the man away into the corridor. The stranger rolled and came up into a crouch, and Jack noticed that his slug had left a large hole in his double's belly, but no blood was visible in and around the wound.

The ship bucked, rising and falling as it spun helplessly in the storm. Jack staggered in the doorway, kneeling down to retrieve the stolen Colt. As he did so, the double pulled his own replica pistols from their holsters. Jack felt much better knowing that this thing wasn't able to produce projectiles to match its outward appearance. It was as if every measure of the facade was for show, like a stage or movie set, the guns merely non-functional props.

"What do we have here?" Deadeye mused, holding his own sidearm level at the twin versions of his captain. "Looks like a pair of Jacks."

The doppelganger laughed. "Good one, Deadeye. Now help me disarm this thing."

Charlie shifted his gaze to Jack, eyebrow raised. He could see blood oozing from a puckered gunshot wound to the left bicep. He staggered in the engine room doorway, jaw swollen and discolored, lip split.

"He can't shoot, Charlie," the real Jack explained. "He's just an image of me."

"Shoot him, Charlie," the double urged. "Quick, before he kills us all."

Then Deadeye noticed the hole in the double's abdomen, and the lack of blood around it. Adjusting his aim, Charlie's .45 rang out, and another hole appeared in the doppelganger, this time its chest.

The ship heaved, then dropped, and Jack felt his right knee give way to an explosion of pain. He crumpled forward to all fours. Sparks retreated back a step with the socket wrench, recovering into a combat-ready crouch.

Deadeye tried to wave her off. "Sparks! No! Wrong one!"

As the *Daedalus* shuddered and shook, the double slammed into the chart room door and bounced back into the passageway, sprinting toward the main saloon. Jack rolled onto his back, his knee and shin throbbing in agony. Instinctively, he reached toward the wound, dropping both pistols to the floor. Sparks furrowed in sympathy, crouching down and dropping the wrench beside him.

"Oh no," she winced, unsure of how best to handle the situation. "Captain, I'm sorry!"

Jack clenched his teeth and nodded after Deadeye, who had already bolted in pursuit of the double. "Go after it!" he growled, angrily enough that it set her head on straight.

"Yessir!" she hissed, plucking one of the . 45s from the deck near his left shoulder, which was now soaking the deck panels red with blood.

Sparks tripped to a halt in the open area just behind the bridge. Three square tables used for eating and lounging stood welded in place by the gondola walls on either side—two on the right side, one on the left, nearest the galley. Six padded aluminum chairs lay strewn across the deck.

She saw Deadeye as he bolted through the forward hatchway toward the cockpit and made a ninety-degree turn left. Boots clanged on metal rungs and Sparks realized Charlie was chasing the captain's double up the ladder to the main gantry. Running fore and aft down the center of the ship's perforated skeleton, it was an open catwalk for maintenance of the gas ballonets, and for accessing the two smaller cruising engines on either side of the envelope.

Sparks paused only momentarily as the ship was shaken by another gust of storm winds, then turned back for the aft access ladder. There was every reason to believe whatever this being was, it might try to double back to finish off the real captain, or completely destroy the engine dynamos.

As she passed the crew quarters on either side of the corridor, she racked the slide back to make sure a new round was in the chamber. Suddenly she found herself at the bottom of the access ladder, opposite the chart room and just forward of the aftmost floor hatch. The circular hatch itself was flush with the floor, with manual and electrical controls buried in the deck plating.

Jack had staggered upright, and limped his way to the hatch controls, using his remaining Colt as a counterweight to help drag his injured leg.

Sparks saw him fumble with the electronic controls and rushed to help. "There's no power to the drop ladder, if that's what you're thinking..."

Jack shook his head. "No," he grunted, every move a herculean effort. "Just help me get the hatch open."

Together, they fished the winch-style crank handle from a round indentation in the hatch itself, pulling it in a circle until the latch snapped back, and the hatch cover tilted up on its lower hinges. A dark whirlwind boiled beneath the ship, the air whistling eerily in from outside.

Jack limped back to lean against the starboard supply room wall, while Sparks kept vigil from the door of her own quarters, also on the starboard side. Both faced the ladder, each with one of Jack's nickel-plated Colts trained on it.

The sound of boots on metal treads echoed from above, and before they knew it, Charlie clambered down into the corridor. "Did you see it?" he asked earnestly, gently grasping his black Army sidearm.

Jack scanned Charlie's torso and noted that he sported a large, open belly wound, without so much as a drop of blood around or inside it. This was the creature's failing: it could reproduce the likeness of an object, but no secondary characteristics, like bullets; it also couldn't hide structural damage.

Jack's Colt blazed until it clicked empty, and Sparks likewise emptied the magazine of Jack's other sidearm, exploding chunks of moist, clay-like flesh.

The duplicate staggered backward against the ladder and the port supply room, various likenesses warping and flashing over its face and body as it smacked against the wall again and again. Deadeye suddenly appeared down the ladder, gripping the outer guide rails with his feet. The moment his boots hit the deck plates, his own pistol flew to his doppelganger's face, and he pulled the trigger.

The homunculus screamed in otherworldly torment as its left eye exploded, fragments of damp clay spattering behind its head across the corridor wall. Its image of Charlie faded, and the creature began to shrink to its original size.

Thinking fast, Charlie seized the doll-like construct and fell forward chest-first onto the deck, hurling the invader through the bottom hatch and out into the storm, where an unyielding fate awaited it a mile down.

Jack took a heavy step forward and pushed the hatch closed with his wounded leg. He took a breath, looking first at Sparks, then at Deadeye.

"Well," he huffed. "That's that. Now let's get this bird fixed."

Suddenly Cipher's voice crackled over the comms. "Captain," she warned, a tinge of terror in her voice, "enemy fighters approaching."

- CHAPTER 16 -

"Stay close to me, Ellen!"

Doc gripped her daughter's coat in her left hand, urging her along at a jog. The foursome navigated completely by memory and the occasional silhouette against the stormy afternoon sky. She peered over Banks' shoulder into the blustery wind and rain, just discerning the outline of the bunkhouse. It was dark, and thus far they hadn't seen any hint of the green-eyed *draugr*.

Something snarled to their right, and Doc realized she'd thought too soon. Three pairs of pinpoint lights stared bright green from the darkness, and suddenly the air around them was a whirlwind of gnashing teeth and bony, talon hands.

Doc set her fire poker at a defensive angle, allowing the armed men in front and behind the space to defend the group. Banks leveled his revolver at a shadowy shape resembling a head and pulled the trigger. The shot blew out a section of the *draugr*'s skull, and it withdrew into the storm with an animal shriek.

The attack made enough of a gap to step through, MacLennan firing twice at the ravening duo behind them. The ghouls slowed but kept up their pursuit.

The group of four sidestepped their way around the rear corner of the bunkhouse, keeping its timber walls to their backs, limiting their enemies' angles of attack. Another ninety-degree turn and Banks flung open the door, stepping inside with a sweep of his sidearm to make sure the coast was clear.

Doc ushered Ellen into the cabin next, checking over her shoulder to see MacLennan focused on a cluster of green lights in the distance. "Hey," she said, nudging his right shoulder with the handle of the iron poker, "inside."

Once within the relative protection of the bunkhouse, Banks set about securing the entrance, while MacLennan lit a single kerosene lamp and set it on the floor for a general-purpose work light. Doc handed the fire poker to Ellen, heading to the pile of baggage and non-essential crew possessions stowed during the weapons test.

Digging her worn canvas duffel from the pile, Doc pulled the tension bead away from the leather mouth of the bag, reaching inside for a particular cedar box. It was quickly located, being heavy and rectangular, its grain red and rippled. Flipping up the latches at each end, she opened the case and beheld her prize: a bronze armor piece—a vambrace for the arm, sized for a member of the ancient female warrior sect devoted to Athena.

Ellen's eyes grew wide in the suddenly piercing light from the lodestone, which bled through her sweater. She'd seen the vambrace before, but never witnessed her mother use it. She knew it had been a gift from AEGIS patron Marina Stavros in Athens, but not how impossibly old it was, or what it actually did.

Laying her left hand on the artifact as it remained cradled in the cedar box, Doc closed her eyes and spoke a short incantation over it. "*Athiná me prostatéfsei sti máchi.*" The inscriptions immediately began to sparkle and radiate a brilliant aquamarine glow. Simultaneously, ringing with a high-pitched harmonic tone, the lodestone in Ellen's shirt swelled with bright light, creating an icy sensation on the young girl's skin.

Without further ado, Doc lifted the armor piece from its silk bed within the case, sliding it over her right arm. Reaching deeper into the duffel bag, she produced a small ammo box, followed by a leather gun belt and holster. It contained a Colt Police Positive revolver, her favorite sidearm due to its ratio of stopping power to recoil—or relative lack of it.

She turned, strapping on the gun belt and leveling a serious glare at the two men near the door. "Okay, gents," she sighed. "Almost ready. Next stop, the armory."

"Armory," MacLennan repeated.

Banks looked over the bronze vambrace, which was still crackling with that same blue-green energy from the invocation. "So, uh... what's that do?"

"It should help protect us from those things outside."

"Looks like it might protect your right arm, and not much else," Banks muttered dubiously.

Doc unholstered the Colt and flipped the cylinder to the side. Thumbing open the small cardboard box, she grabbed a handful of 38-caliber cartridges. Within seconds, she'd slotted six into the revolver and pocketed the rest. Then, with a flick of the wrist, she snapped the cylinder back into position. "You're gonna have to trust me on that," she admonished, moving toward the door with the pistol held low.

Ellen maintained a close position behind, gripping the poker with both hands. "You'll have to trust her."

"I'll take point again," Banks volunteered, but Doc was already shaking her head no.

"Not if you want the armor's protection," she said.

Banks scowled. Gender notwithstanding, Doc was a civilian, and he was uncomfortable with *any* civilian standing at the front of a dangerous situation. Then again, he wasn't altogether sure what kind of training these AEGIS people received, so the term "civilian" might not have been completely accurate.

Doc pulled the door open and stepped out into the storm, followed by Ellen with the iron poker, then Banks and MacLennan.

The ghastly mob was on them immediately, all snapping teeth and slashing, clawing fingers. Glowing eyes stared out from dead, dark sockets. Desiccated flesh stretched over gray bones, almost invisible in the dark and the flurry of the savage attack.

Doc led with the Colt in both hands, letting the monsters come to her. The first wave broke on the group like winter surf, withered talons and skeletal limbs repelled in mid-assault. The foursome was suddenly awash in an explosion of aquamarine light, then another. Each pulse rippled out across an invisible, spherical cushion of space around them.

Banks exchanged a look with MacLennan. Each raised an eyebrow, impressed.

Still the mob forced its attack. Limbs flailed as the ghouls slashed at the huddled group of mortals. Storm winds howled, merging with the hisses and snarls of the undead. Pulse after pulse washed over the group like a bioluminescent fireworks show.

Backtracking toward the armory and Banks' office, each of the three adults fired a few rounds into the snarling mass of monstrous creatures, working their way slowly through the courtyard with the swirling wind and rain in their faces. Ellen, already competent with some rudimentary fencing moves, supplemented their gunfire with jabs and stabs from the middle of the group.

Squinting through the misty darkness, Doc could see the main mob of perhaps a dozen creatures was coming into position by the armory door. Two individuals stood in the rear of the mass of Arctic ghouls, their silhouettes full and faces dark, with no green glow present in their eyes.

One of them is Corporal Stevens, she thought. *Not sure of the other, but whoever it is might be controlling the horde.* She began calculating and discovered their number of rounds compared to the number required to neutralize even a single *draug* was alarmingly low. "Fellas?" she addressed. "The armory might be off the table."

Banks was clearly following a similar train of thought. "Corporal Stevens!" he bellowed over the screaming winds. "What's the meaning of this? Stand down!"

A lone voice from the rear of the mass of glowing eyes and jagged gray bones cried out in response. "Oh no, I don't think so, Sergeant-Major! The Master will decide what to do with you!"

"The Master?" Banks hissed to his companions.

MacLennan leaned in close enough to be heard. "Aleister Crowley. He runs this bunch."

"This bunch?" Banks repeated, his thoughts circling like marbles in a glass jar. "What...um, what's—"

"The *Astrum Argentum*," Doc said matter-of-factly. "The Silver Star society."

MacLennan found himself playing out their possible moves in his head. The armory was looking very much like a non-starter, much as Doc had posited. "Back to the main office, then?" he asked.

Banks ignored the suggestion, yelling back at the assembled mob of *draugr*. "Stevens, this is your last chance! Stand these things down and surrender, or face the consequences!"

"No dice, Banks!" came the reply. "Now say your silly prayers to whichever silly god you pray to."

Doc frowned. Their only shot at stopping these creatures was to neutralize the living entity or entities controlling them, but the *draugr* made a very effective screen. Then Stevens cried out over the storm once more, and a chill shot up her spine.

"Kill them!"

ʘʘ

"Don't kill them," Shaw instructed to the assembled strike team. "At least try not to."

The vacant hangar at Cricklewood was lit with the warm glow of carbide work lamps above. The same eclectic group from the tarmac earlier in the day was gathered inside, out of the cool, moonlit night: the blind Hell-fighter, the android, the disfigured Gurkha, and the Roma tracker. They numbered one more now, the French girl who had arrived in the coffin, standing among her compatriots with a cocky stance and sassy attitude. She cut an androgynous figure—all the rage in Paris these days—with her short-cropped raven hair and men's suit vest and trousers over a tailored blouse. She wore black wingtips on her feet, and a matching black fedora at a jaunty angle on her head.

"Don't know that we'll have much choice," the pale woman answered in a Parisian accent with a throaty chuckle. "I hear they burst into flames or some-such."

Shaw frowned. "You're thinking of vampires," he corrected with a dry half-smile and a...was that a wink? She couldn't quite tell. He did only have one eye, after all.

Joe Desmond spoke from the back of the group, arms crossed, leaning against a workbench. "The average Silver Star agent is subject to the Soul Contract, wherein if they are captured or killed, their life essence is transferred to Crowley or one of his close lieutenants for use in their own magicks."

"Thank you, Seer. Now, let us remain on topic," Shaw said, turning to the rolling chalkboard behind him. On it was drawn a rudimentary floorplan of the townhouse on Green Street. He gestured with an ancient wooden school pointer, explaining each step. "Now, Mila's intelligence indicates the primary ritual chamber is the main floor conservatory, but we would raise too much public suspicion going in through the front door. We'll drop you in from the roof, and you can make your way down from there."

Mila raised an eyebrow at Abhik Bhandari, the Gurkha, who shrugged in response. He was used to clearing bunkers and trenches in brutal hand-to-hand combat. Clearing a few bedrooms and paving the way for the others didn't seem like an insurmountable chore.

Shaw cleared his throat. He was beginning to have second thoughts about the operation. These people had only been on a handful of missions thus far, against extremely soft targets. Now they were going after Crowley himself?

"If I may, Colonel?" Desmond stood from his leaning position and ambled to the front of the room. "Durgasur, you're leading the insertion from the rooftop. There's a skylight into one of the studies up there—that's your entry point."

The Gurkha nodded silently. He respected Colonel Shaw as a top-level planner, but Desmond had been "in it", as they say. He was a natural when it came to leading a small team on a specific mission.

"Evelyn-4 follows," Desmond continued. "Mila, you cover any escaping agents from the rooftop."

The young Roma nodded, content. At last, something was happening.

"Vamp," Desmond said, "you gain entry from the north side. Use one of the dormers."

Therese grinned, elongated vampiric canines visible in the acetylene light.

Desmond pointed at a drawn square on the rear of the floorplan. "And I will enter here, at the conservatory."

"Our target," Shaw reminded them, "is Crowley and his inner circle. Subdue them if possible. We will have the police standing by."

The hive-like hum of turbofans became gradually louder and closer, coming to a slow halt outside the hangar.

Joe Desmond grinned. "I think our ride is here, folks."

"Alright, ladies and gentlemen," Shaw announced. "Get your gear and get out to the tarmac. The *Percival* will take you to your objective."

- CHAPTER 17 -

Three Heinkel HD 38 biplanes roared past, lightning painting their black finish in a flash of white. Jack, Deadeye, and Sparks stood absolutely still as the storm hammered on the side of the ship's envelope. Finally the growl of the fighter planes disappeared, merging with the roll of thunder in the distance.

"They didn't see us," Jack realized. "Not in this soup. We just stole back a minute or two of vital time."

Deadeye noticed Jack was favoring his battered knee and his left arm was soaked with blood. Charlie's own head throbbed, and it looked like Sparks had a similar experience as well. This was not a crew at their very best.

Dhakiya pulled the bandanna from her neck and knotted it around Jack's left bicep in an effort to staunch the bleeding.

Jack spoke first as he let his engineer wrap his upper arm in the cotton cloth. "Sparks, I need you to fix whatever that thing did to the ship. Bring the power systems back on. Weapons first, then engines. Then we'll track down the mechanical problem with the launcher."

"Aye, Captain." Sparks nodded. "Sorry again about the knee." She left her first aid handiwork and headed back to the engine room hatchway.

"Deadeye," Jack continued, "topside...try to get the Hotchkiss guns warmed up, keep those fighters off us. I'll see if I can find any gas leaks or other damage." The wind rattled the deckplates again, and Jack sighed. "We just gotta stay alive up here as best we can."

"Is that all?" Deadeye asked, somewhat sarcastically.

Jack shrugged. "Gonna have to be, for now. If we can get the radio detector and the rocket launcher up and running, then maybe we can do something. But right now we're fish in a barrel." The hallway shook with another swell of wind, and he added, "A really shaky barrel."

With that, Charlie clambered back up the metal ladder to the gantry above, while Jack hobbled forward toward the bridge.

The outside of his right shin throbbed with every step, and his knee kept threatening to collapse under his weight. The loss of blood from the bullet wound in his left arm wasn't exactly helping matters, either. The short stairway from the main saloon into the bridge access felt like summiting Everest.

"Cipher," he panted, hanging onto the railing with failing strength. "Need some help."

His vision clouded momentarily and everything spun, but Jack reckoned it was just the storm, batting his ship around like a cat playing with its food. In the distance, he heard the drone of airplane engines pass by again. So far, they hadn't spotted the *Daedalus*. Every moment that was the case was another chance to repair the damage to the ship and fight back.

Jack suddenly felt arms around his ribs, guiding him to the pilot's seat. He allowed himself to sit, gliding with an exhausted grunt into the welcoming leather cushions. This was good. This was familiar. He could fly this ship in his sleep. His vision cleared almost immediately. He was sitting at the helm, Cipher's dark eyes staring into his.

"Captain…sir…"

Jack tried to shake his mental cobwebs loose. Reaching up to wipe something from his eyelids, he realized his face was completely covered in a sheen of sweat. He winced with the stab of pain that raced through his arm and neck as he pulled the flight yoke into place. "Help Sparks," he ordered. "Gotta get the ship's systems back up."

"But sir—your arm, you've lost blood…your leg…"

"I can still fly this crate," Jack growled. "Even winged like this."

Cipher winced, but ultimately decided that his current condition was not the hill she wanted to die on. Jack McGraw was famously stoic in situations like these, and had flown the last two incarnations of this ship with an assortment of fractures, abrasions, and holes in his body. Not all at once, to be sure, but there was a reason they usually had to re-upholster the pilot's chair after every mission. He tended to bleed through them.

"Aye, sir," she acknowledged, helping place the wired headset on his sweaty brow.

As soon as Cipher left his side, the radio detector blinked back on, sending its waves out like rings in a pond. Jack heard the approaching roar of the Heinkels and their water-cooled V-12 engines, and prepared to maneuver as they swarmed overhead.

But before he could adjust altitude, the chugging cadence of the quad Hotchkiss guns erupted overhead. He heard one of the BMW engines sputter and drone away toward the open water below. *Charlie got one,* he thought. *Either Sparks restored power to the turret, or the fighter happened to fly in front of the guns. Either way, score one for our side, and I'll take it.*

He shook his head again to clear the remaining fog, and suddenly the cabin lights came up, then dimmed to normal cruising brightness. Glancing at the console, he saw the engine gauges ping back to life, one after the other. Total power capped off at 82 percent, which told him at least one of the dynamos remained damaged. Even so, it was enough juice to maneuver on.

"Bless you, Sparks!" he shouted to the empty bridge, nosing the ship down into a dive. He felt the subtle vibration of the outboard turbofans spinning up, and the hydraulic whine of the lateral controls at his feet.

At least now he could mount some resistance to the storm.

At least now his barrel of fish was a bit less shaky.

As the ship banked downward in one of Jack's favored corkscrew maneuvers, Deadeye felt the giant thrusters rev to life. He could tell they weren't at full power, but anything was better than getting tossed around like a lacrosse ball. Finding the second fighter in his targeting reticle, he gripped the triggers on each side and let the incendiaries fly. He heard the staccato rhythm of the Hotchkiss guns as they blasted red tracers into the wind and rain, and the stutter of the fighter planes' machine guns in response. The incoming tracers were green, as Charlie was used to. One random round ricocheted off the turret canopy, skipping into the air. Another penetrated the envelope directly in front of him, but at such a shallow angle he doubted any structural harm was done.

As the biplane sped ever closer in its run across the spine of the *Daedalus*, Charlie caught the massive BMW engine in his crosshairs and—

Thud-thud-thud-thud-thud

The Hotchkiss spewed red fire at the incoming enemy, culminating in a colossal explosive display as the engine compartment ignited. One half of the spinning propeller sheared away and tore through the tail assembly before trailing off into the vermilion sky. The rest of the burning plane spiraled down into the Strait of Georgia.

Two down, he thought. *One more in this squadron, and three more beyond that,* if the support capacity of the supercarriers remained unchanged from when they last encountered them. The odds were still not stellar, but they were improving.

Then a flak cloud erupted along the spine of the *Daedalus*, and Deadeye saw a section of its coated metallic skin begin to peel away in shreds.

Oh, damn.

The *Daedalus* bucked and fishtailed sideways in the storm, and Jack cursed at the flight yoke as he fought for control.

"What the hell?"

He immediately pulled back on the stick, terminating the dive and reversing it, then banking in a hard right turn. His pilot's intuition had served him well in prior combat situations, and it told him that if his craft was hit, change the current maneuver. If the attacker was leading fire, a sudden alteration in course would help separate the two and put the enemy off-target. The impact had been in the port side, so his instinct was to pull away from the shot's point of origin.

They were climbing again, thanks to the maneuvering thrusters. But the swirling red maelstrom pounded the envelope on all sides, and a steady barrage of flak from the *Osiris* kept them from any safe harbor in the sky.

"Damage report," Jack grunted into the radio. "Anyone. What's it looking like?"

Charlie's voice crackled into his ear. "Uh, we got a nice hole in the outer skin, Cap'n. About the size of a manhole cover. Doesn't look like the ballonets were hit."

Jack glanced over at the console and confirmed gas pressure was unchanged. "Received. Thanks, Charlie. Keep an eye out for those fighters."

"Affirmative."

As the comm channel closed with a static *click*, Jack straightened the turn and continued climbing. They were only at four thousand feet, and he knew if they didn't at least try to get over the mass of the storm, they'd be finished. How high it extended, he hadn't a clue. The *Daedalus* had an "official" service ceiling of twelve thousand feet, but he'd taken her as high as sixteen thousand and change, instinctively knowing she'd go higher. Perhaps not enough to get over a storm of this magnitude, but they'd never know unless they tried.

Then he caught the hiss of wind through the hole in the windscreen, and he realized they wouldn't be able to keep the bridge pressurized. Feeling just under the left armrest of the pilot's seat, he contacted what he knew to be an emergency oxygen mask. It was a redundancy, tied into the ship-wide O_2 supply. If need be, he could seal off the bridge and wear the mask until the oxygen was depleted.

He reached over to the console and flipped the toggles to purge the last of the ballast tanks, knowing that as he did so, the *Daedalus* became ever lighter and less resistant to the punishing winds.

"Cap'n," Deadeye hailed over the comm channel. "The last fighter has broken off! He's heading back!"

Jack's stomach sank into his boots. He knew when the Silver Star withdrew one piece from the chessboard, it was because they had a much more terrifying piece ready to move. It occurred to him, as he struggled to maintain a stable climb, that the storm was likely too much of an obstruction for a fighter assault, and the *Osiris* commander was banking on superior firepower and the brutality of the weather itself. Jack had piloted planes and airships in tropical typhoons and hurricane winds. This was, by far, the worst storm in which he'd ever flown.

As he continued the climb, Jack said a silent prayer to the god of airship pilots that he'd see Doc and Ellen again.

Then the sky opened with black blossoms of anti-aircraft flak, another section of vulcanized skin torn away. He heard the turret canopy peppered with metal shot as the sound echoed throughout the envelope like BBs in the barrel of an air rifle. A second explosion erupted, followed by the shriek of metal pulled apart.

Jack swallowed. "Charlie," he huffed into the comms. "Charlie, report." Glancing at the console gauges, he saw they were leaking lift gas from ballonet six. "Deadeye, report!" Jack snapped. "Come on, Charlie!"

A third explosion from the aft quarter was followed by a hard blast of wind, and Jack realized the severity of their situation. The *Osiris* was forcing them into the outer arm of the storm cell. The choice was either stand fire and be taken apart by enemy guns or be torn asunder by nature's fury…or rather a fury not found in nature at all.

He fought the stick as the winds played tug-of-war with the wounded airship. "Charlie!" he ordered. "Charlie, respond!"

- CHAPTER 18 -

The mob was a frenzy of bony claws and gnashing teeth, hissing with arcane breath, their eyes aglow with preternatural energy. The creatures swarmed over the group as they huddled together, three adults and a ten-year-old girl.

As before, the *draugr* swarmed them, intent to overwhelm them with numbers. Doc's mystical vambrace kept the attackers at bay for the moment, spasming in explosions of phosphorescent blue-green with each savage strike from the undead horde.

"Stay with me!" Doc demanded. "Keep pushing forward! We're almost to the armory!"

Sergeant-Major Banks fired his revolver until the cylinder clicked over empty. He leaned in close to Doc, producing a handful of rounds from his pocket and reloading. "Yeah, but what then?"

"Let me worry about that when we get there!"

MacLennan fired his own sidearm point-blank, tearing away bits of bone and fibrous flesh from the attackers, but nothing stopped them completely. Their process was slow, and he had no idea how long Doc's magical defense would last. He needed to do something to change the parameters of the fight. He sighed as his own revolver gave up its last round into the snarling mass of dead faces.

A volley of automatic gunfire impacted the protective shield, rippling across its surface like raindrops in a pond.

Doc scowled. Some son of a bitch had an MP-18. She should have known. It was really par for the course with the Silver Star. She let out a small, silent laugh, thinking their situation might have finally become untenable.

Before she knew what was happening, MacLennan bolted from the group, sprinting into the storm and the darkness.

"MacLennan!" Doc screamed after him.

Banks joined in, squinting through the wind. "Inspector!"

Ellen watched, both troubled and intrigued by the gambit as she struck out randomly with the iron poker.

Whatever MacLennan's plan was, he took it with him as he bolted toward a section of barracks. To the group's collective surprise, the mob peeled off in pursuit, hissing into the darkness after him.

There was a brief scream of pain and anguish over the howling wind, then the storm sang on alone.

With the *draugr* gone, Doc could now see the two figures limned in the lantern light from the armory. Corporal Stevens stood with a pistol raised to elbow height and the grin of someone hollowed out inside. Next to him, holding the trench sweeper, was Captain Ecke. She recognized the bushy white sea captain's beard and officer's cap.

The force field suddenly flickered and evaporated, the carvings on the vambrace went dark, and Doc knew they were out of time. "Shit," she sighed, pulling Ellen close behind her.

Corporal Stevens raised his revolver to fire, and a shot rang out.

Doc winced in anticipation of a bullet that never pierced her frame. Opening her eyes, she watched Stevens slide down the armory wall, a crimson trail descending from the exit wound in the back of his skull.

Banks recovered from his shot, tilting the still-smoking barrel skyward. Then he leveled the weapon again, lining up a shot at the bearded officer, and thumbing back the hammer.

Doc raised her own revolver and cocked the hammer in unison with Banks. She felt Ellen tug at her jacket and glanced down to see her daughter nodding behind them.

The *draugr* had finished with MacLennan and now surrounded their rear flank, cutting off any means of escape.

She gasped in horror.

The dead husk of Captain Hummel, the *Schwarzhund* of the Silver Star, glared at her with that familiar green glow of eldritch light. The last time she'd seen him, he'd fallen beneath the Arctic ice.

Standing next to him, hunched like a giant suffering under his own weight, was their erstwhile benefactor, Sten. Member of a lost Viking enclave, Sten had fought alongside Doc and the crew in the battle over an alien orb with the power to resurrect the dead with a radio pulse. Killed during the fight, he had been raised to be used as a weapon against his former comrades.

Doc had seen him go down on that burning ship, sinking below the frozen waters of the far north. Yet here he was, back again, lifeless but for the otherworldly magic animating his frozen corpse.

The undead gathered in a semicircle behind Banks, Doc and Ellen, ready to attack.

Sergeant-Major Banks and Doc Starr took aim with their revolvers.

"Drop that heater, mister!" Ellen demanded.

Ecke blinked in the dim amber light, and Doc cleared her throat.

"Ellen, honey..."

"No, Mom," Ellen pushed back. "You can shoot each other, or you can shoot him and the ghouls get us. Either way, no one wins."

The various parties exchanged puzzled glances.

"It's a stalemate," Ellen added, referencing her chess terminology. "The only way we all don't lose is for him to surrender."

Doc nodded, recalling their last encounter with Captain Ecke on the *Luftpanzer II* over Sanctuary Island. She and Jack had let him go. She wondered if he was an honorable officer who would return the favor, or the typical Silver Star operative who would sabotage everything simply to join with the Master when all was said and done.

"Red's right," Banks said, tilting his head to glare at Ecke through the darkness.

The sudden clatter of metal on dirt made the trio jump. The trench-sweeper lay in the wet dust at Ecke's feet.

"*Ja,*" the captain nodded solemnly, raising his hands, palms out in front of him. "She is right."

Banks hesitated. "Am I correct in assuming you're giving up?"

"I wish to…*was ist? Ja.* Defect."

Doc's head swam. Captain Jonas Ecke, the most effective airship captain in the Great War, commander of two iterations of Aleister Crowley's flagship, was surrendering? Laying down arms? Coming over to their side?

It had to be a ruse.

"How can we trust you?" she snapped, surprised at her own rancor.

Ecke's face was granite. "I still control the horde. I haven't ordered them to attack you."

Banks broke away from Doc and Ellen, moving toward Ecke to better survey the situation.

"How do you control them?" Doc demanded.

"May I?" Ecke asked, keeping his hands visible and bowing slightly.

Banks approached quickly, keeping his sidearm trained on the older man. "No tricks," he warned.

"No tricks," Ecke repeated. "Like the *Mädchen* said, you could shoot me, but the horde would kill you, and nobody wins."

As they watched, Ecke reached into his trouser pocket and produced a smooth, green stone.

"If I wished, I could make them attack now..."

The trio tensed as the captain spoke, Banks shoving the barrel of his revolver into Ecke's ribs.

"But I offer the stone to you, *Doktor*," he said softly, bowing his head reverently. "You are a well-known and respected occultist among the *Astrum Argentum*."

Well-known, maybe, Doc thought. *But 'respected'?* She cast a backward glance at the assembled corpses as they swayed in the blustery breeze, awaiting command. "Whatever this magic is," she said derisively, "I want no part of it."

"You heard the lady," Banks grunted. "Shut it down."

Ecke shrugged in a slow, exaggerated motion. "Very well." Placing the stone in his left hand, he clasped his right hand over it and pressed the palms together. His eyes closed for a moment, and he breathed a deep sigh.

As they watched, the *draugr* collapsed into the pile of lifeless dead flesh and bones they'd been before their unwilling reanimation.

Captain Hummel.

Sten.

Every last glimmering emerald eye went dark.

- CHAPTER 19 -

Maria gazed out through the array of tempered glass panes on the *Osiris* bridge, watching the spiraling maelstrom below. Her eyes blazed red with eldritch fire. She could feel the exchange of ethereal power running from Crowley through her, into the eye of the storm, and back to her. Power on a scale she'd never experienced, even during her year navigating her "hell dimension". She could feel her master metaphorically behind her, focusing his power through her like sunlight through a magnifying glass. She knew he was receiving his own trickle of arcane power, but only as much as she allowed.

The lion's share she kept for herself. Where it belonged.

The supercarrier hung suspended in the sky above the storm, her engines keeping station. At an altitude of 18,000 feet, all personnel were restricted to their duty stations, mostly in pressurized cabins. Those working in non-pressurized areas were equipped with personal oxygen tanks and masks.

The radio operator, a Serbian woman with jet black hair pinned into a tight bun under her service cap, put her finger to the headset. "We have lost two of the first flight, but have isolated the approximate location of the *Daedalus*!"

"Call back the last pilot," Maria ordered. "And continue firing in that area." Her eyes became slits leaking unholy crimson light. "Either we will rip them apart with our guns, or the storm will do the same." As she watched the center of the storm expand like a red sun, her lips turned up in a ghastly smile. "Or the Elders will consume them."

◈

"I'm okay, Cap'n."

Deadeye staggered in the bridge doorway as the *Daedalus* tossed and spun, manhandled by the brutal wind currents outside. Blood ran from several gashes on the side of his head. "Last shot took off the turret canopy. I managed to slip my harness in time." He reached up to feel his temple, returning fingers stained with red. "Topside's open to the weather now."

"Charlie! Thank God you're okay!" Jack turned in the pilot's seat, still wrestling the flight yoke with his right hand. Noting Deadeye's condition, his brief smile turned to a grimace. "Crack a first aid kit and see to your head, buddy. When you go, seal the hatch to the bridge. Then help Sparks if you can. We need that launcher up and running!"

Deadeye gave a halfhearted salute and stumbled aft, slamming the aluminum door to the cockpit and spinning the lock wheel until it stopped. He threw a final look through the tiny window and then stepped away, leaving Jack alone on the bridge. Angry winds whistled through the bullet hole in the front windscreen. The hole itself had sprouted fingers which extended out in random spider web cracks. Too much more stress and they'd lose that windscreen panel.

"Sparks," Jack wheezed into the comms. "When you get a moment, hit the oxygen. I'm gonna need it to fly us anywhere more stable." Fumbling for the mask with his injured left arm, he managed to drop it a couple of times before draping the strap around his neck and letting it hang on his chest. He'd be able to feel when the air started to flow.

"Aye, Captain," Sparks replied only moments later.

The ship shuddered with another gust of wind. Jack fought to steady her. His vision blurred for a moment, and he felt an old panic well up in his gut—a panic he hadn't really felt since the war.

"Hitting the O_2 now." Sparks' voice in his ear was a soothing tonic.

A high-pitched hiss began to emanate from the mask under Jack's chin, and he felt the cool wash of air across his sweaty face. Pulling the mask over his nose and mouth, he pulled the strap tight at the left side and let go, inhaling fresh oxygen. His vision flushed red momentarily and then became suddenly vivid. His mind gradually cleared of cobwebs.

A blast of wind bludgeoned the nose of the ship, and the windscreen panel shattered, falling away into the storm. Wind whipped savagely at Jack's face, and he clumsily grabbed at the flight goggles resting on his forehead, pulling them into place over his eyes as he continued to battle the ship's controls.

They were in the most turbulent zone of the storm, the "eyewall" in hurricane terms, although this was no normal hurricane. As lightning arced through the sky ahead, Jack throttled up and continued the climb. A storm's center was usually calmer and less chaotic than the outer bands. If it were at all possible, he would find the eye of this storm.

They might be safe there. For awhile, anyway.

☞

"There's good news and bad news," Sparks announced to her crewmates, as the flexible walls of the airship continued to vibrate with the onslaught of the wind.

Deadeye frowned. "Always good news first," he said, a bit louder than intended.

Cipher examined her handiwork as she reapplied the bandages to his head. He'd made a mess of them the first time around. "Always," she agreed.

Sparks looked up from the breech of the missile launcher, Deadeye and Cipher watching from the main saloon a few steps above her. "The good news is I've located the problem with the launcher."

Deadeye nodded, following along. "What is it?"

"Whatever that thing was must have lodged a foreign object in each tube." Sparks tapped a pair of pliers on her grease-stained chin. "I can see them. There's nothing wrong with the power system. The problem is a physical obstruction."

Cipher's eyes grew wide in happy anticipation of perhaps not dying today. "So if we clear it..."

Sparks bobbed her head in the affirmative. "And we really only need one functional tube to work."

"So let's clear it," Deadeye clapped his hands together impatiently.

Sparks took a deep breath and sighed. "That's the bad news," she replied. "I can't clear it from in here. I'm gonna have to go outside."

"What?!" Cipher exclaimed, mouth hanging open.

Deadeye tried not to shake his head. It made him dizzy. Nevertheless, he didn't feel so good about Sparks' idea, and made it known with a low, loud, "*No.* Absolutely not. Even tethered. The storm is kicking the piss out of us. It's too risky."

"Then *what?*" Sparks demanded, standing in the small well aft of the former nose turret. "Our only other guns are at the bottom of the Strait of Georgia with the dorsal turret! We just have to remove the obstruction in *one launch tube*, and we'll have a functional weapon!"

Cipher placed her hands on her hips, cocking her head to one side. "Sparks, that's not the part of the equation we disagree with."

"How are you gonna stay attached to the ship and be able to work?" Deadeye demanded.

Sparks almost laughed at the way the two of them were standing, like concerned parents, quizzing a daughter going to a dance with a partner of questionable background. "If the captain can get us into a zone of more docile winds, I won't have to be attached."

◌

Jack inhaled the piped oxygen and wrestled the flight controls in a passive turn, drafting in the prevailing wind current and allowing it to push the ship in a wide corkscrew motion upward. They were at 14,000 feet and climbing. Power readings were nominal, although one section of batteries was fluctuating on and off.

Probably damaged when the turret canopy was blown off, he thought.

The cockpit frame shuddered against a crosswind, and Jack adjusted for the disparity. The turbulence continued down the frame of the airship, rattling cables and deckplates. Weld points cried out under the strain.

Icy spikes of freezing rain shot through the open windscreen panel and splatted on his goggles. Wiping them with his wounded left arm was agony, but he managed a smudgy pass before something in the dark distance caught his eye. Perhaps a mile out ahead of them, a warm red glow began to penetrate the arms of the storm. Jack angled the outboard thrusters and throttled up to cut through the maelstrom's last inner walls. Even if it wasn't the true eye, it was a focal point, something he could use to navigate.

All of his internal warning bells, based on thousands of hours of actual flight time, were going off like high noon in a clockmaker's shop.

Red skies at night, he recited in his head, *sailors' delight.*

Red skies at morning, sailors take warn-ing.

Jack wasn't sure which applied here, as the storm had come up suddenly in the middle of the day. He decided, between deep breaths of pure oxygen, that he would add to the old mariner's rhyme.

Red skies at noon, probably doom.

Jack chuckled into the breathing mask. He was no Keats, but it would suffice.

The battered airship jumped and rattled once more, vulcanized fabric skin flapping. Jack realized his trousers were soaking wet and frozen at the knees from the rain coming through the gap in the cockpit window array. On the other hand, the inability to feel his right knee he took as a blessing.

A wall of wind slammed into the *Daedalus* head-on, sending its nose into the air.

And then—nothing. Winds slowed. Lightning ceased. For the first time in half an hour, the flight yoke wasn't fighting him.

They were through the last storm wall. They were in the eye of the storm. Probably.

There was no sign of the *Osiris*, nor its fighter escort, thankfully.

Jack scanned ahead beyond the rain-streaked windows. The distant ethereal red glow had not been an optical illusion. If this was truly the eye of the storm, there was something at its center he'd never seen before, except maybe atop that temple in the Amazon, when Aleister Crowley attempted to summon the demon Choronzon.

But this roiling bubble, this rift in space, was larger. Much larger.

Jack took a station-keeping position a mile west and a few thousand feet above the crimson eye at the core of the storm, watching it boil and ripple, sending shockwaves out into the pulsating storm. He estimated it to be probably a half mile across, with a bulbous center like a swollen eyeball or alien egg sac.

And wriggling within that translucent red amniotic sphere was a collection of dark reptilian or piscine tentacles, each impossibly long, flexing against the thinning membrane to be released.

I don't know what those belong to, Jack thought, but I don't wanna stick around long enough to find out.

- CHAPTER 20 -

"Why aren't you dying?" Doc demanded, peering through squinted eyes at Captain Ecke.

The old airship commander sat at a small desk table in the corner of the armory, as the storm continued railing outside. His hands were folded together, and he faced his captors calmly. Although he'd considered defection more often since the failed siege of Noble's Isle in 1927, Ecke had never quite assembled a finished plan. He knew only that, of all the AEGIS personnel to surrender to, the airship *Daedalus* crew were his best option. Most of them were veterans of the Great War and had that nobility of character associated with the conflict. They respected their fellow combatants and adhered to the rules of engagement.

Crowley felt no such compunction, and so Ecke's years in his service had begun to sour. This was far better, he assured himself. He would be treated fairly, and could debrief without divulging any state secrets, as the *Astrum Argentum* was not a recognized nation.

Banks leaned against the timber wall, one hand resting on his holstered revolver. He was sure this uniformed officer was someone of great importance to AEGIS. Nevertheless, this fort was under RCMP jurisdiction, and he was the sole authority here right now.

Ellen jawed a fresh piece of Beeman's gum, sitting on a stool beside several stacked ammo boxes, tapping the floor with her fire poker. Doc paced the room, trying to get what she could from their erstwhile adversary, as quickly as possible.

"*Was?*" Ecke frowned. "Oh, the Soul Contract."

Banks furrowed his brow. "Soul Contract?"

"Acolytes of the Silver Star must submit to the Soul Contract," Ecke explained. "It is a mystical bond which allows Crowley—or sometimes Maria—to absorb their life force at any time."

Doc shuffled her boots on the worn, wooden floor. "It's why we've never been able to capture one of their agents alive," she added. "But it still doesn't explain—"

"In the wake of the Great War," Ecke continued, "I was recruited to command the flagship of Crowley's army. He needed my expertise more than my life essence. Some ranking officers in the organization are not subject to the Contract."

"Ranking officers," Doc repeated. "Like Maria?"

"*Ja,*" Ecke replied. "Like Maria. *Und* Captain Hummel, outside."

"Yes, we first encountered him in Greenland."

"Indeed. In life, he was the *Schwarzhund*—the Black Dog—of the *Astrum Argentum.* Brash as a commander, but I respected him as a gentleman."

Doc threw him a glare, and he realized he was veering off-topic.

"Er, there is a scientist, Himmler, and various field commanders. Mercenary cohorts, personnel of that nature. Highly-placed contacts, like your Corporal Stevens. None are required to make the pact."

"Highly-placed?" Banks laughed. "Corporal?"

Ecke looked at the Mountie and uttered quietly, "He had you fooled, did he not?"

"Interesting promotion track they've got," Banks said, addressing the room. "Advance high enough and you won't have to worry about having your essence drained away, but if you die, we'll bring you back as...whatever those things were."

"*Draugr*," said Ellen, matter-of-factly. "Viking undead."

Banks' eyebrows crept upward on his forehead. "*Viking*...undead." He glanced at Doc, extremely unsettled that a little girl would know such information. "How oddly specific."

"They're an eclectic organization." Doc pursed her lips together, anxious to get to the meat of the interrogation. "What was your ground operation? Looks like you were targeting the armory. What was your goal?"

"I was tasked to lead this unit of *draugr* to the armory and take your supply of the experimental rockets."

"And Corporal Stevens was your inside man."

"Correct."

"This stone," Doc said, indicating the flat jade rock in her hand. "What's it do?"

Ecke swallowed. "Gives control of the *draugr* to whomever carries it."

"But they're neutralized now, right?"

"*Ja.*"

"What is this?" Doc asked, tilting her head toward the window, and the swirling storm outside the tiny cabin.

Ecke frowned, not understanding.

"The storm, Captain," Doc reiterated. "This is not a natural phenomenon. Is it cover for your ground operation?"

"Partly," Ecke admitted. "But it appears to be a summoning beyond anything the Silver Star has attempted before."

Doc blinked, and the color left her face. "Summoning. What kind of summoning?"

Banks shifted uncomfortably. He hadn't known Doc all that long, but the one thing he did know about her was that she was darn near fearless. Something that made her go pale like that was not something to be ignored. He glanced outside, noting the appearance of several flashlight beams crisscrossing in the dark. "Looks like my boys are back." Moving to the door, he exchanged a look with Doc. "I'll be right outside. Holler if you need any help."

Doc nodded politely, waving him away so her captive could continue. Then Banks was gone, shutting the door with a *thud*.

"I don't know the details," Ecke admitted. "I am kept out of much of the arcane plotting. But I can tell you this: Maria went missing for over a year, after the summoning on Noble's Isle. When she resurfaced, she had...new knowledge. New powers. And Crowley took advantage of them for his own edification."

Doc set her jaw, fury in her eyes. "That woman has been trying to summon eldritch terrors as long as we've known her. And those spider-demons almost overran the island because she couldn't control them. We understand you are using these things as a new power source?"

Ecke nodded silently.

Doc took a deep breath trying to calm herself. "Alright, Captain. What 'new powers' does she have, and what are she and Crowley up to?"

Ecke ran a gnarled hand slowly through the bristles of white beard. As good as it felt to come clean, he couldn't help but wonder how much Crowley and his minions were monitoring the interrogation. It made him err on the side of quiet candor. "They are working in concert. Maria can open portals large enough to transport a ship like the *Osiris* across spatial dimensions. And working through her as a conduit...an amplifier for his own power, Crowley can conjure this storm."

"I don't understand," Doc began. "It's a storm. Jack's flown in conditions nearly as bad."

Ecke shook his head with certainty. "I guarantee you, he has not."

"Damnit, Ecke," Doc snapped. She was suddenly in his face, slamming her fist on the table in front of him. "What aren't you telling me?"

The officer looked at her with weary blue eyes. "The storm is a by-product."

"Of what?" Doc demanded.

"Of what is at its center."

Doc glanced at Ellen, and back to Ecke. A windowpane rattled in a gust of wind. She bent forward, arms braced on the table, looming over the airship captain. "*What* is at the center?"

"At best, madness," Ecke said, a tear escaping his eye and disappearing into his whiskers. "At worst, annihilation."

⌘

"She's doing what?" Jack exclaimed over the comms, his voice muffled by the oxygen mask and the whistle of gentle wind through the cockpit window.

Cipher's voice was calming, despite the desperate situation they found themselves in. "Sparks says she needs to access the launch tubes from outside the ship."

Remembering the escape hatch under the pilot's chair, Jack pinched the *TALK* button again. "Hang on. We could rig a safety harness, and cable her down from the emergency hatch."

"We already thought of that," Cipher answered. "No good. It drops her too far away from the launch tubes, and we'd be without flight control if anything happened."

"But we haven't tested those jetpacks yet!"

"Someone at the AEGIS Science Division did. And the Valkyries have been using them for over six months now."

"I wish they hadn't changed our loadout," Jack complained. "We were trained on the old gyro-packs."

"A gyro-pack wouldn't be able to clear the underside of the bridge," Cipher reminded him.

He couldn't argue the logic. Sparks was right, and Cipher was right to defend her position.

"I just wish she had some training and flight time."

"Time is one luxury we *don't* have. We're going to have to trust her, Captain," Cipher urged. "The dorsal turret is *gone*. The Hotchkiss guns are *gone*. It's the only way to bring *any* weapon system back on the line."

"And the sooner the better, in that regard," Jack sighed. "Okay, tell her to be careful."

"Affirmative," Cipher replied, signing off.

As Jack held the flight yoke in position, he watched the viscous orb at the center of the storm's eye and shuddered. Even from this distance, he could see movement within the vortex. A blood-red tentacle pressed at the cell wall, stretching the dimensional membrane with a flex of unearthly sinew. His throat filled with bile, a primal revulsion. He hated to think what he'd be seeing without the clarity of the oxygen.

Whatever we do, he thought, *we'd better do it fast.*

❧

"Are you sure one of us shouldn't take this mission?" Deadeye asked, hefting the jetpack strap over Sparks' right shoulder. "Cipher and I both have flight time on the gyro-pack. You didn't even get that."

The two stood in the aft cargo bay, strangely spartan as it was, having been relieved of extraneous gear to keep weight minimized.

Dhakiya Kitur, Kikuyu princess, gazed hard into Charlie Dalton's eyes with an intensity he'd rarely seen from anyone beside "Captain Stratosphere" Jack McGraw.

"My purpose on this crew," she said, "the job I was hired to do, is to keep her flying and safe. She's flying at the moment, but she is not safe. I am the only one qualified to make the repair."

"You're not trained on this thing," Deadeye warned.

Sparks rolled her eyes. "Neither are you, genius. And we need you to operate the weapon and Cipher to work the radio guidance. Now grab that helmet for me."

Deadeye plucked the crash helm from the wall hook. Hefting it in his hand, he realized it was made from the foam-steel AEGIS had pioneered back in '26. Light, yet far more durable than vulcanized rubber or canvas. He handed it to her, running through some rudimentary pointers. "Okay, throttle control is on the left strap, up front here. It's a single thumb lever. Ignition is right below it. Make sure the throttle is down when you hit it, or we'll be peeling you off the cargo bay ceiling."

Sparks nodded, following along as she pulled the helmet over the bandanna covering her braids. "And steering is with the body," she added, fastening the strap under her chin. She twisted at the middle, waggling the two stabilizing fins on the outside of the twin air chambers. "I did read the manual."

"Yes ma'am," Deadeye continued. "Any slight turn or flex is gonna change your direction, so be careful."

Sparks adjusted the weight of the pack so that her hips took the majority, then turned back to Deadeye. "Give me a minute to get used to the flying part," she instructed, "then be ready to load and fire those rockets we have left."

"Affirmative," he replied. "You've got return points here in the cargo bay, at the side gondola doors, the top hatch, and both bottom hatches. But make no mistake. If we encounter problems, don't be afraid to head back down on your own."

Charlie looked her over, noting the tools on her mechanic's vest were all tethered with thin rope of a soft cotton/hemp blend. A small gas welding torch hung from the front right side of her belt. "Best of luck, Sparks," Dead-eye said, clapping her on the shoulder and stepping over to the large, red, industrial button that raised and lowered the *Daedalus'* aft cargo ramp door. "Ready?"

Sparks lowered the flight goggles over her eyes, then slipped the oxygen mask over her head and took a breath. Her gaze dropped as she examined herself down the front. She was pretty sure she had everything necessary to get rid of whatever had clogged the missile launch tubes. She told herself that if she could clear both tubes easily, she would. However if the wind picked up or if something else happened, one functional launch tube was better than no tubes at all.

She nodded. "Ready!"

Charlie secured his own oxygen mask and hit the button. A spiraling amber warning light began spinning in a slow circle, in unison with a klaxon bell. The only time the rear cargo ramp was lowered while in flight was when people were coming or going, so all hazard protocols were in play. The ramp began to lower on hydraulic pistons, the cargo bay suddenly awash with the ambient red glow from the eye of the storm. A mild wind whipped around them.

When at last the ramp was lowered far enough, Deadeye gave Sparks a thumbs-up and stepped away from the door controls.

Knowing that any delay would only compound her fear, Sparks took a breath of oxygen from her mask, made three steps forward, and fell into the crimson sky.

- CHAPTER 21 -

Maria shuddered, suddenly aware that the stone commanding her *draugr* had been deactivated. Whether the creatures themselves had been destroyed or the stone had been removed from Ecke's possession and disabled, they were no longer on the chessboard. The void of their presence, the emptiness, was tangible, but now Maria had a modicum of extra power at her disposal. Reaching out with her purest will, she felt the energies realign, and a new boost in the fount from Crowley, channeled through Maria, into the membrane at the eye of the maelstrom. Soon, very soon, their cosmic "egg" would hatch, letting a particularly monstrous brand of chaos and horror loose upon the world.

She spared only the briefest thought, wondering as to the whereabouts and condition of Captain Ecke, before casting it aside, refocusing on the eye of the storm.

"*Meine Führerin*," cried the operator at the *Osiris* radio console. "We have sighted the *Daedalus*. They have pushed through the storm wall and are currently below and opposite the vortex from us."

Maria stood in place behind the map table on the bridge, viewing the endless skies through the window array. Her eyes radiated with the same eldritch fire. Her mouth, already a menacing smile, broke into a malevolent grin. "What is their condition?" she inquired, relatively sure she already knew the answer.

The raven-haired radiowoman pointed delicately to her earphone, listening to the chatter over her comms. "Observation reports they are heavily damaged."

"Excellent," Maria said softly. "Gunnery stations, prepare for bombardment."

A young man with cropped blond hair and a black officer's jacket stood near a console with various targeting data and a radio handset for communications with the gun decks. "I'm sorry, *Meine Führerin*, but they are below our firing arc. Perhaps we can move closer—"

"Do not move position!" Maria ordered with grave finality. She paused briefly, then: "Scramble the second wing. Our fighters should be able to fly within the eye of the storm. Shoot that airship down, or force it within our firing arc, or force it into the portal. Any of those three outcomes will suffice."

"*Jawhol, Meine Führerin*," another lieutenant on the bridge replied, plucking a handset from a nearby console and barking some orders in German.

Maria felt the ominous surge of ethereal power as she watched the dance of writhing tentacles within the transparent orb at the center of the storm. She spoke in a hushed tone, for herself and no one else.

"Today I will see the end of Captain Stratosphere, and the *Daedalus* crew."

CR

When Dhakiya Kitur was a little girl, her father would hold her by an arm and a leg and swing her around in dizzying circles. She would squeal in that mixture of childhood fear and delight, and they would both ultimately collapse in a fit of laughter. At the time, that was as close to flying as she came. Then, during secondary school, she'd gone to work as a mechanic at the RAF airfield in Mombasa. But even that job didn't allow for actual flight experience, despite the proximity to a host of British Army planes.

She'd been so busy keeping the kites flying that she'd never had the opportunity to go up in one.

Now, she flew. Not gracefully at first, but in the halting fashion of a first-time automobile driver. It was intense and liberating and absolutely terrifying. She corkscrewed toward the clouds making up the inner storm wall of the eye, then realized how far below the *Daedalus* she was. Shifting her hips beneath her, she throttled up and angled toward the nose of the small airship.

As she approached from below, she glanced across at the pulsating rift at the center of the storm for the first time, watching fingers of red lightning escape and palpate among the clouds. She saw the writhing mass of blood-colored eldritch flesh within, flexing and pressing at the membrane.

Suddenly a single eye appeared—an ancient, yellow, inhuman eye. It blinked open, pressed against the transparent barrier, quickly scanning all around. Then it shot upward, catching Sparks in its glare.

A primal chill shot down her spine.

In the distance, a formation of three Heinkel fighter planes closed the distance.

They needed to get out of there, and fast.

From inside the gondola, Deadeye heard the *clank* of a metal clip secured to one of the many exterior safety handles. Hefting one of the small guided rockets into his hands, he waited for Sparks to clear the obstruction.

"Going to the bridge," Cipher informed him. "I'll guide it to target."

Deadeye winked, but inside he was a nervous wreck. "Affirmative."

A mild breeze pushed and tugged at Dhakiya's uniform and mechanic's vest. One cable was hooked to the handle of the emergency hatch under the bridge, another to the side of the front turret, replaced as it was by the rocket launch system. With one booted foot on the canopy and the other across the launch tubes, she looked like a mountaineer in mid-ascent.

The blue-white exhaust from the twin jets on her back glowed soft and low, at zero thrust. Sparks clutched the handle of her welding torch and twisted the gas on, unable to hear the hiss from within the crash helmet. Flipping the cannister down and behind her, she ignited the torch with the jet exhaust and bent to heat the interior of Launch Tube A.

When she felt the metal was hot enough to soften whatever the homunculus had crammed down the barrel without damaging the launch tube itself, Sparks shut off the welding torch and returned it to her belt. She produced a pair of pliers from her vest, reaching deep into the barrel and grabbing onto something that felt like a random shard of aluminum. Just enough to gum up the works.

With a slight turn of the wrist and a kick from her boot, it popped free, and she let it fall from the pliers' teeth, into the swirling abyss.

CR

Edward "Duke" Willis steadied the fight controls as he throttled down, and the airship *Percival* came in over Green Street, London. The moon had risen but was hiding behind a gauzy blanket of high clouds. Without running lights and cruising at one-quarter speed, it posed no interest to anyone who wasn't specifically looking for low-flying airships over the London skyline.

"Coming in over drop point," Duke said softly into the comms, his voice a posh English baritone. "Ready away team." He flipped a couple of toggles on his console and pushed the headset back on his head with the officer's cap he always wore. Without thinking why, his mouth cracked a wry smile, making his black pencil-thin mustache form a V-shape. Although he was commander of the *Percival*, he hadn't actually flown her in some time. His Australian pilot, Sheila Barrett, was usually in the pilot's seat. However tonight's mission was more of the "off-the-books-personal-favor" variety, as opposed to official AEGIS business. AEGIS was, after all, supposed to work in accord with the various allied governments. It wasn't so farfetched an idea that *one* AEGIS reconnaissance airship and pilot be made available for an MI-6 operation in London.

In the main saloon, Durgasur prepared his line. His uniform was of a green and gold Hindu motif, with brass studs and a hooded cloak. A bronze mask of the demon that was his namesake covered his patchwork face, projecting a fearsome grimace. Two small *kukri* daggers were sheathed on his belt behind his back. Two larger ones, each about the size of a pirate cutlass, were housed in scabbards at each hip. The cable he attached to his belt allowed for a quick, controlled descent and instant release once on the ground —or in this case, the roof.

Evelyn-4 scanned the open aft belly hatch with electronic eyes, testing her own cable line.

The forward floor hatch also lay open. Mila stood at the ready, having already been secured for several minutes.

Vamp had changed into black motorcycle leathers and a long overcoat. She winked at her Roma teammate, then turned to their unit leader, Joe Desmond—callsign Seer. "See you on the other side, *mon ami*." She found Mila's gaze again and broke into laughter. "I jest! He cannot see!

Desmond, clad in dark leather and flowing robes, stood by the open side gondola door, blind white eyes staring out across the city. "I see clearer than you, *cherie*. I see truth." He turned toward the saloon interior, addressing his team for the final time. "Remember: we need Crowley alive. Despite what Shaw says, the rank-and-file agents are on borrowed time already, so do as you will. See you down there."

With that, Joe Desmond stepped out into the air.

Durgasur took a small jump through the belly hatch, keeping his limbs locked in tight. The android medic followed, then Mila through the forward exit. Vamp was the last to leave the *Percival*, becoming a cauldron of flapping bats which soared into the dark night.

The London night air was cool and misty, as they descended at about half the speed of freefall. After only a hundred feet or so, boots hit slate roof tiles, and cables released. The bats swooped and swarmed, reassembling into the form of Therese St. Claire at the north end of the roof. Durgasur and Evelyn-4 rushed quietly to the large skylight on the south side, while Mila took up position behind a dormer facing the street.

Joe Desmond descended like a divine creature, hands held flat with palms downward, controlling his fall with sheer willpower. His hooded robes and cloak billowed out like ghostly wings. He came down in the back garden just outside the blacked-out conservatory window, broadcasting with a single thought to each of his teammates.

Now!

- CHAPTER 22 -

Sparks located Deadeye through the canopy window and flashed a thumbs-up at him, then cocked the same thumb to her left.

Deadeye returned the gesture and hefted the radio-rocket in his hands. She'd cleared Launch Tube A. Now was the time to put it to use. Deftly slipping the missile into the open breech of the mechanism, Charlie slammed the cover down and thumbed the *TALK* switch on the intercom panel next to the cannibalized nose turret. "Rocket in the pocket, ready to fire."

Over the speakers, Deadeye heard Jack's ebullient voice give the firing order. "Target *Osiris* aft hangar. Fire at will, Charlie!"

In this case, *at will* meant *right the hell now*, and Deadeye knew it. He punched the fire control and watched out the window as the rocket shot out into the vortex, streaming fire from its tail.

On the bridge, Cipher sat hunched over the communications console, monitoring the radio detector. She breathed slowly and steadily into her own portable oxygen mask, drawing from a cylinder strapped to the small of her back. "Sir!" she warned, her face a puzzle of emotion. "I don't have a lock—no, belay that. I have it now."

Jack made a slow pivot around the nose of the *Daedalus* to track the missile, watching its vapor trail. "You've got the hangar?"

Cipher squinted at the detector screen, watching its green readout shift with every electronic sweep. "I'm not sure," she said. "I think so. But there's some interference coming from the rift."

As the rocket passed in front of the bulging membrane between the *Daedalus* and the *Osiris*, it suddenly banked left, impacting the portal. The explosion was catastrophic and sent a shockwave surging outward that knocked Sparks away from the airship's nose. Fingers of lightning arced into the clouds as an impossible, unearthly groan erupted from within the cell. The sound was like the death of some great colossus, piped through a thousand tube amplifiers. A massive coil of tentacles spilled into the sky over the Strait of Georgia.

Sparks throttled up and angled back, just as one of the liberated tentacles lashed out, coiling around the *Daedalus* bridge.

Three fighters passed overhead, machine guns chattering.

The ship lurched forward, dragged by the demonic appendage and perforated by enemy guns, and Jack muttered under his breath, "Shit."

"Cap'n?" Deadeye's voice buzzed in Jack's earphone. "We're taking heavy fire and we've only got two more rockets! Suggest we make good use of them!"

Jack throttled full reverse, straining against the coil of demonic sinew that had ensnared his ship. It wasn't working. Nothing was. Sooner or later—probably sooner—the *Daedalus* was going to get pulled through the broken membrane, into some hellish dimension. A dimension from which they would likely never escape, not that they'd live long enough to worry about it.

And that was if the fighter planes didn't completely chew them up first.

He looked at the gas gauges on his console and his stomach sank. Another ballonet was penetrated, leaking precious helium-hydrogen compound.

Cipher cast a worried glance at the pilot's seat. "Should I target the eye?"

Jack's mind raced, trying to break through the fog of pain and blood loss. They could expend their last two missiles trying to fight whatever uncanny terror currently had their ship, or go for the power source that had summoned it. "Negative!" he ordered. "Keep locked on that aft hangar bay and give it both rounds!"

Deadeye's voice was resonant. "Rocket ready, Cap'n!"

"Fire!"

The gray-white exhaust trail probed out ahead of the *Daedalus*, Cipher guiding it above and over the portal as the demonic lasso tugged at the tiny airship. It hit an apex and then arced over, shooting down on the rear section of the supercarrier with incredible speed.

It impacted the outer roof of the *Osiris* flight hangar and exploded, starting an intense chain reaction: airplane fuel ignited, then diesel reserves, then the aft engines themselves. The massive zeppelin began to swerve and drift. Heat shot through copper wiring like a jolt of internal lightning, and the first section of hydrogen ballonets erupted in a *whoosh* of fire.

The three fighters banked in formation, circling back around to make another pass.

"Captain," Cipher hailed. "Permission to use the last round—"

"Do it, Cipher!" Jack ordered, leaning over hard with the flight yoke. We can't lose another ballonet!"

Cipher hit her *TALK* switch. "Deadeye, load the last rocket and fire!"

"Firing, aye!" came the reply, tinged with static.

Cipher tracked the tiny blip on the radio detector and plotted the guidance, bringing it nose-up and around to face backward. The fighters came in an arrow formation at full speed, hoping to rip open the spine of the *Daedalus*.

As the lead fighter's guns opened up in a shower of green tracer fire, the final rocket screamed through its engine compartment, tearing the cockpit and pilot in two. The propeller spun away, and the left wingman barely dodged in time to avoid it. The exploded plane rolled directly onto the right wingman, consummating their union in a fireball of death.

The left wingman rolled away from the *Daedalus* and the explosion of metal, canvas and fuel, looking for a way out of the storm. The second section of ballonets on the *Osiris* were aflame, shooting charges of burning hydrogen in a telltale *chuff-chuff-chuff* sound that terrified aeronauts of any nation. There was nowhere to land on the supercarrier. She was foundering.

Straight down seemed to be the best option, perhaps even a water landing...

A red tentacle shot suddenly and viciously from the rupture in the eye of the storm, slicing the small plane in half. The pilot began to dissolve in midair, his essence called home to the Master as the wreckage of the fighter spiraled into the dark below.

As Jack watched, the massive envelope of the *Osiris* began to bend and buckle, caving in on itself in the aft quarter. He grunted, still fighting the controls and the eldritch beast pulling them toward the portal.

A purplish lightning bolt ran down the arm of the elder god, followed by another unnatural scream. Jack automatically glanced upward, though the bridge position under the nose meant he couldn't see what was happening topside.

What he couldn't see was Deadeye, cabled to the dorsal hatch door, hefting the ship's lone Tesla rifle and taking aim at the giant appendage wrapped around the ship. He blasted again, sending a powerful arc of electricity at the crimson tentacle, opening a second smoldering wound. The second time was the charm, and the Old One retracted its arm into the portal, its primal shriek echoing into the heavens.

Sparks throttled down, lowering onto the top of the *Daedalus* envelope. Deadeye put out his left hand and she grabbed it.

As the two stood atop their tiny floating island in the storm's vortex, the swirling cloud wall began to break up. More tentacles erupted from the portal, but all of them latched onto the *Osiris*. The giant ship groaned as more hydrogen gas bags exploded, and massive demonic arms wrestled the ship out of the sky, snapping the structure in half.

Like a child's toy sucked down a sewer drain, the *Osiris* was pulled into the portal, into the dimensional door at the center of a storm which was now blowing itself out. A roiling, growling peal of thunder erupted on shredded sound waves into the atmosphere, and the membrane sealed as the portal closed in upon itself.

It was suddenly, eerily quiet. The only red light left in the sky was the natural effect of a beautiful western sunset, as the first evening stars began to twinkle above in a curtain of deep blue.

Their numbers were M-772 and M-815, respectively. Their given names were offered up with their souls when they'd signed on with the Silver Star. They were young, clean-cut lads—one Hungarian, one Romanian—who appeared almost as identical twins in their black uniforms, MP-18s and matching field caps.

From the moment the glass from the skylight crashed in to the time Durgasur landed on the floor with two gleaming blades, they barely had time to utter a gasp of surprise or register their disbelief.

In the following three seconds, neither one of them had the opportunity or the will to do much but fumble with their weapons as the demon in green slashed through their bodies like a scythe through wheat. They were dead before their brains knew it, and began to smolder and dissolve almost immediately as their spirits were called home to merge with their Master.

The android descended into the room, tiny jets of thruster fire erupting from her legs to slow her fall. "The alarm has been triggered," she informed her partner.

"I assumed so," Durgasur growled, heading toward the door into the stairwell down.

"Do you require medical attention?"

The question was so bizarre and ill-timed, it made the ex-shock trooper pause. He looked back at the construct and cocked his head, presenting a rather comical effect with the frightening Hindu mask.

Evelyn-4 returned the head tilt. "Repeat: Do you require—?"

"No," Durgasur huffed. "Now come on."

On the roof, Therese St. Claire hefted the window sash and winked at Mila, who was covering her position with the scoped rifle. "A kiss for luck, *cherie?*"

Mila shot her a savage look with dark eyes.

Therese feigned shock. "No?"

"No."

"Pity." Then she was through the window and disappeared within the cavernous town-house.

Down flights of stairs she sped, half running, half flying. Although the alert had been sounded, every Silver Star agent she encountered seemed shocked at her very presence. Two, four, then six—she slaked her thirst at their open throats, often coming away with a mouthful of smoky ash as they dissolved.

Durgasur and Evelyn-4 descended the stairwell on the south side of the house, Abhik's slashing blades cutting through their opposition, who crumbled and burned away before they fell to the floor.

This was a skeleton crew. A minimal defense.

Outside, Colonel Shaw paced Woodstock Road in front of the police paddy wagon. To any outsider, it appeared a quiet, still night. He wouldn't know if the mission had been a success until the team informed him. He flicked a stainless-steel lighter and lit up a cigarette, taking a long draw and questioning his infatuation with the costumed vigilantes as the future of AEGIS. Field teams with the paramilitary training provided by the organization made for more efficiency, to be sure. Doctor Starr probably had studies and data to that effect. And yet...for Shaw, it was more about providing opportunities to people who had been given the smelly end of the bog stick.

People like Durgasur, and Vamp. People who, if left alone and without aid, might end up on the wrong side. Who might require a more thorough intervention later. No, he'd keep backing this play.

As long as they didn't kill each other in the process.

The green demon and his mechanical partner reunited with Vamp on the second floor.

"Any trouble?" Therese asked.

The man in the bronze mask shook his head. "None. This is too easy."

"Agreed," whispered Vamp. "I'll take the back stairs to the servants' quarters."

Durgasur saluted out of habit. "Affirmative. Meet you in the garden."

Seer stood outside the curtained windows of the conservatory. He could see brief flashes of light within, as if someone were lighting fireworks. But he would never last in a mystical battle against Aleister Crowley unless he shed his material form and presented one of purest will. And that required projection.

Mila, he broadcast to the tracker keeping watch on the roof, *come to the east of the house, overlooking the garden. I need you to keep an eye on my body.*

What are you going to do? she thought back.

I'm going to leave it for a bit.

As Mila crept to the edge of the slate roof, she heard a footfall behind her. She turned, instantly discerning a Silver Star agent and firing her rifle from the hip. The man fell, sliding toward the edge of the roof, frothing and dissolving as he did. There was nothing left to impact the ground forty feet below. She arrived in position and peered through her targeting scope just in time to witness the Seer collapse into a heap of dark robes at the foot of a lone ash tree.

Joe Desmond opened his eyes to a circus of color—a vibrant three-dimensional display of objects and patterns, everything in the material world represented in a rudimentary framework on the astral plane. There was no time to work himself up to confront Crowley. They'd already lost the element of surprise. He gathered every ounce of his willpower and launched his astral form at top speed, through the conservatory windows.

He should have known better. Of course there would be a ward on the ritual chamber, if it were to be protected from psychic incursion. He would have planned the very same security measures.

His spiritual senses lit up like a bonfire, every nerve in his astral body awash in agony. The images hit him in rapid succession, like a boxer's assault. They bludgeoned his mind, one after the other: The bridge of the *Osiris*, with its screaming crew and Maria's furious face staring back at him across dimensions. The heady sensation of drawing her power back away, after feeding her reserves. Taking everything. The deep red tentacles and single, baleful yellow eye, pulsing at the transparent membrane, trying to break through. The snarling mob of *draugr*, tearing a man's guts out of his body, as his piteous screams echoed in Seer's astral ears.

The conservatory portal. The ritual over British Columbia. The assault on the RCMP fort. The storm. It was all a trap.

It had always been a trap.

Any single element could have worked—any or all, in fact. But like a professional gambler, Crowley always left an emergency exit. And it usually put him in a better strategic position than when he'd started.

Very good, Joseph, came a nasally English accent in his head. *You found me. But don't get used to it.*

The room was spinning. Seer clutched his skull in absolute torment. He managed to raise his eyes just for a moment, and caught the smiling, round face of The Great Beast of Mankind, as he slipped through a portal and closed it down. *I must be off, but I'm sure we'll see each other before too long.*

Suddenly the pain ceased. The colors and lights stopped flaring, the images in his head stopped flashing. All was quiet.

The conservatory was littered with random ceremonial objects, now used and powerless. The ornate sigils and chalk circles had been smudged and broken. A few random piles of robes and ash represented where Crowley's closest acolytes had been stripped of their essence. The faintest scent of ozone and candle smoke was all that remained.

"Palm trees," Joe Desmond muttered as his sightless eyes fluttered open. His compatriots gathered around him, concerned as Evelyn-4 assisted him to a sitting position.

They were next to the police wagon on Woodstock Road. A unit of uniformed police went over the townhouse, bagging, cataloging, photographing.

Colonel Shaw puffed on his cigarette one last time and stomped it out on the sidewalk. "What's that, Desmond? Palm trees?"

Desmond grunted, blinking the dust from his blind eyes. The brief link with Crowley's mind had been illuminating, but full of ego. Had he truly foreseen the arrival of The Altered at the house on Green Street? Or did he just have a remarkably convenient escape plan? Was he really a three-dimensional chess master whose strategies rivaled those of Lao Tzu? Or did he just get more inventive and aggressive when painted into a corner?

"The portal he used to escape. I think...I think he's in Tunis."

- CHAPTER 23 -

The *Daedalus* descended softly in the fort parade square at Gibsons Landing. Unlike their first arrival, this time the area was crawling with Mounties, and they'd brought out diesel generators with temporary work lights to help in the rescue effort.

The moment the airship touched down on solid ground, Jack McGraw took a deep breath of piped oxygen, and passed out.

He awoke in the fort infirmary an hour and a half later, left arm in stinging pain but dressed and secure in a sling. His right knee felt like it was on fire. Glancing down, he saw that it had been set in a temporary splint.

Doc's emerald eyes greeted him with a sparkle he hadn't seen in awhile.

"You look like you have a story to tell," she purred softly.

Had he ever missed those green eyes and that gentle bedside manner. The thing about Doc that made her one hell of a field medic was that she instinctively knew when she could be a bit tougher with you, or when to treat you with kid gloves. When the team was taking fire and she was patching up wounds temporarily, she could be, as their former mechanic Rivets used to say of Edison, "a real hard-nosed sonnovabitch". No quarter given when everyone had to keep their collective fists up. It was when the fighting was over that she became a sanctuary and would spare no comfort for her patient, especially when that patient was also her lover and partner.

Jack smiled, but it looked more pained than happy. "Boy howdy. And you guys?"

"We had a time of it," Doc admitted sadly. "MacLennan. He...he didn't..."

"What happened?"

"*Draugr*," Ellen announced.

Jack turned over to see his daughter leaning her elbows on the cot. "You okay, Red?"

Ellen smiled. "Pff. Of course. Those things don't scare me."

"She did you proud, Captain Stratosphere," Doc smiled. It was a sad, resigned, exhausted smile. "And Captain Ecke defected over to our side."

Jack's left eyebrow shot up. "Really." There was a long pause, his mind filling with volumes to say on that matter. The commanding officer of the Silver Star's aerofleet? Defected? What was the angle here? What was Ecke's play? Or Crowley's? He opened his mouth several times to begin his lecture on the topic, but decided to conserve what little fuel he still had in the tank, uttering a simple, "Huh."

Sergeant-Major Banks entered through the door, doffing his Mountie hat. "Evening, Captain," he said formally. "If you're mobile, the seaplane's ready for you. Everyone else is aboard. Not that I'm anxious to be rid of you... but I'm anxious to be rid of you."

Jack glanced around the small building for the first time, noting that he was the only living patient. A few bodies took up beds opposite him, covered in wool army blankets. "Who's that?"

"MacLennan," Banks answered. "Corporal Stevens. Turns out he was one of the baddies."

"Sten," Doc added.

Jack gawped at the mention of the name. "Sten? How?"

Doc patted his chest, shushing him. "I'll fill you in. We'll have plenty of time on the flight back to Los Angeles."

Jack began to shift in bed, but there was still more to discuss. "What's going on with the *Daedalus*? How is she?"

"We're getting her repaired." Banks rotated the brim of his hat between his fingers. "Your Lieutenant Commander Singh will be piloting it back to Seattle."

"It's actually Commander Singh now," Doc sighed. "She wanted to tell you when this mission was done. They've given her the *Vayu*."

Jack tried to push himself upright, and Doc and Ellen helped him.

"Holy cow, how long was I out?"

Doc laughed, happy to have Jack back alive, and in one mostly-reparable piece. "Quiet, you. Let's get you out to the plane. You're gonna be off that leg for a few weeks after surgery, so we can catch you up on everything. And you can tell us all about flying in that storm."

With Doc under one arm and Banks under the other, Jack limped out to the harbor, where he was then carried to the plane by a few Mounties from the local unit. Cipher met her crewmates at the dock, giving each a warm embrace and promising to come visit soon.

"Congrats, Commander Singh," Jack whispered as she hugged him.

Her dark eyes lit up and she leaned in for a soft peck on the cheek. "Thank you, sir. I wanted to tell you—"

Jack shushed her, holding up his good hand. "No need, Commander. All is well," he said with a wink. He began to duck through the entry hatch but turned to regard Cipher again. "I'm gonna miss you at those comms. And as a pinch-hitter at the helm. But I'm thrilled that you'll be leading your own crew. You've proved more than capable over the past few years." He nodded, adding, "Best of luck with the new command."

Ellen hugged Cipher around the waist and pulled away, saluting. "Fair winds, Commander Singh!"

"Keep up the good work, Red," Cipher grinned. "You'll have your own command before AEGIS knows what hit them."

Ellen ducked inside the amphibious plane, leaving Cipher and Banks watching their departure from the wharf.

Deadeye and Sparks were already aboard and asleep. Doc frowned as she got Jack and

Ellen situated. "Gonna have to wake them every couple hours. How did they both manage to get their bells rung that badly?"

"A little critter with a mean pistol-whip," Jack replied.

Doc blinked, then her smile returned as she took her seat next to him. "Oh, this had better be one hell of a story."

Jack reached his right hand over and found Doc's left in her lap. "Like you said, we're gonna have some time. Just us, by the pool. And *no missions*."

"Amen, brother."

"But maybe a little derring-do..."

Doc feigned a shocked look, gazing into his eyes with a playful scold. "Captain McGraw, what did I say about derring-do?"

Jack winked. "Um, that you enjoy it immensely, and will only engage in it with specific ruggedly handsome pilot..."

"Don't push your luck, Captain Stratosphere," Doc closed her eyes and leaned back on the headrest as the seaplane began to taxi.

Jack chuckled to himself. *Nah,* he thought. *There's been enough pressing of luck lately. Mine and everyone else's.*

"Hey dad," Ellen chimed, turning in the seat in front of her father to get his attention.

"Can I fly the Fleetwing while your leg heals up?"

Jack shut his eyes as well, mimicking Doc. "Don't push your luck, Red."

Ellen huffed, returning to face front.

Jack and Doc simultaneously opened their eyes and exchanged a look.

"What?" Jack shrugged.

"Don't look at me," Doc said, returning to her resting pose as the plane took off into the night sky over Western Canada. "She's *your* kid."

◌

Mila watched the afternoon sun suspended in the sky over the tarmac at Cricklewood. She wore the same long leather coat, the same wool *šajkača* hat. After months in the field, she'd finally had a good scrub-down bath and her clothes had been laundered. At the very least she no longer smelled like an army barracks in the summertime.

An airliner was due any moment to take her back to the Continent, where she would begin tracking Crowley all over again. To say she was angry would have been an understatement, but she kept that anger purring in a cast iron boiler in her heart, its energy to be used when she needed that little edge to help her out of a bad situation.

Colonel Shaw was not the object of her ire; he'd let her in on the operation to apprehend Crowley, who had eluded them. It wasn't his fault. Just the private little fortunes of a private little war. But rest assured the next time she had The Great Beast of Mankind in her rifle sight, she wouldn't hesitate to pull the trigger.

"Back to Paris, then?" a voice hailed from the broken concrete behind her.

She turned to see Joe Desmond approaching. He wore civilian street clothes: a gray twill suit and matching fedora. As he arrived at her location, he dropped a large US Army duffel bag at his feet.

Mila nodded, her broken English laced with spite. "Yes. And then to Tunis." She had to look away. Joe's white, sightless eyes were still unnerving. And yet, the way he navigated the world without a cane or any artificial aid... was he truly blind? Or was it merely a different way of seeing?

"I can't guarantee that it was Tunis that I saw," Joe said. He let a moment pass before adding a clarification: "But my hunches are rarely wrong."

Mila hefted the leather rifle case in her hand. "Nor is my aim," she said, not with hyperbole, but as simple fact.

"Do you want to tackle this on your own?" Joe asked. "Or would you like some help?"

Mila turned suddenly and met Joe's empty eyes. "We...you don't have orders...what of Colonel Shaw?"

Joe grinned. "Stephen Shaw is a reasonable man. If we provide adequate intelligence, he'll usually give us the go-ahead. And if the adequate intelligence comes in the form of a completed objective...well, let's say he's a man who knows the value of begging forgiveness over asking permission."

A freshly-restored Bréguet 26T airliner circled in for a landing, its tail painted with the Bahamian Blue Ensign—a field of blue with the Union Jack in the upper left corner. It was met by a small team of mechanics in coveralls, and a fuel truck to replenish its tanks. As the technicians did a brief inspection, Joe noticed something on the gleaming white fuselage: *BONNET AIR TRANSPORT* in black letters, punctuated by the image of a small pirate flag.

The rasp of wheels rolling on concrete erupted from within the old hangar into the afternoon sunlight. Abhik Bandari, in a white cotton traveling suit and khaki Australian slouch hat, pushed a black lacquer casket on a rolling dolly. He wore a plaid scarf around the lower half of his face, covering his nose and mouth. The android Evelyn-4, in a complete civilian disguise with long coat and cloche hat, scuffled close behind him.

"Well, well…" Joe mused. "Look who else is going to Paris."

Mila glanced behind her, then exchanged a look with Joe, her eyes bright.

The former Harlem Hellfighter gave her a wink. "I'm sure it's just a coincidence."

- CHAPTER 24 -

Los Angeles, December 1929

The October stock market crash had been a scary moment for many investors, especially those on the AEGIS board with publicly-traded companies. Regular steel production was down, and the manufacturing sector was depressed. Fortunately most of the titans of industry—and their stooges in Congress—had taken a lesson from the smaller slump in March, and put in some temporary fixes to stabilize markets through the end of the year. There were some exciting new ventures between AEGIS and the governments of the US and Britain on the horizon, with talk of manned space flights in the next decade.

Jack and Doc had put all their spare cash into a few British companies developing some of the technology that would be used for such projects, and kept their other investments local, ranging from farms to airplane manufacturers, and even to movie studios. As such, they'd weathered Black Tuesday without appreciable loss.

Various intelligence reports began to filter down to Jack and Doc after their own were filed with AEGIS Command.

Despite the apparent failure of The Altered to nab Aleister Crowley from the townhouse on Green Street, there was enough evidence to suggest they'd interrupted something important, so the team was disbursed with a bonus, and the promise of more work in the future. Crowley had been barred from re-entering Britain, and there was now a rumor being spread among various field operatives that he was in fact a German agent, specifically linked with the growing Nazi party in Germany. He was on the lam, possibly in North Africa.

Colonel Shaw was unaware that The Altered were already in Tunis; had been for months in fact, sniffing around for any trace of Silver Star activity. Sensing a larger coordinated action on the horizon, Shaw immediately began to assemble trained strike teams to be placed around the globe, able to act at a moment's notice, rather than swooping in from a remote location and losing precious days in the bargain.

The *Defensores de la Tierra Dorada*—or DTD—had already been formed to monitor Central and South America. *España el Libre*, "Spain the Free", kept a vigilant eye on the growing fascist movements on the Iberian Peninsula and throughout western Europe. An aerosquadron known as *Huànyǐng,* Mandarin for "phantom" or "mirage", took to the skies over East Asia. The *Walezi* assembled crusaders for justice from across Africa, under the leadership of Bwana Kifo, the skull-painted, unkillable blade fighting avenger the *Daedalus* crew had encountered in Kenya. The *Motu Leoleo*—or "Island Protectors"—brought a roster of Polynesian heroes to the fight, while the Oz Mob watched over Australia and New Zealand. Back in the States, Black Condor's squadron and Red Eagle's Eagle Brood patrolled the Mexican and Canadian borders, respectively. The Regulators patrolled rural backroads in Old West costume, and the Vigil Corps attracted an eclectic lineup of vigilantes from across the west coast.

It was early September before the final operations report from Gibsons Landing was filed, and it left a number of questions unan-swered.

A few cables and brackets from the *Osiris* were the only wreckage retrieved from the Strait of Georgia. The supercarrier was listed as "missing with all hands". Jack reckoned that was generous, considering last he'd seen the ship, it was being bent in half, crammed into the unholy maw of an elder god, sucked into another dimension. Still, Maria Blutig had proved tenacious enough in the past to return despite seemingly impossible odds.

The presence of Sten and Captain Hummel among the other Nordic and Inuit undead in the ground attack on the RCMP fort was evidence that Maria had visited the site of their showdown in Greenland, where they'd secured the alien orb just the year previous. Perhaps she knew it to be a place rich in easily-accessible dead bodies. Perhaps she thought the familiar faces would have a chilling effect on Doc. It was, in the end, a moot point. The inanimate *draugr* were placed on a wooden raft which was set ablaze and towed out into the strait, where it eventually crumbled to ash and fell away into the depths.

Sten had been given a Viking send-off after all.

The *Daedalus* was patched together enough in Seattle to be flown back to West Orange, New Jersey, where it was to undergo extensive repairs and refitting. Upon arrival, Cipher accepted her new commission and took command of the *Vayu*.

Between the bullet wound in his left bicep (his second in as many weeks) and what turned out to be a shattered kneecap, Jack spent the dog days of summer and into early fall off his feet, usually reading a technical magazine or an adventure novel by the pool. By the end of September, his pilot's tan had evened out nicely. Sparks was a frequent visitor to the ranch, sitting with Jack for long bull sessions, or making him Kikuyu cuisine as best she could with ingredients from Southern California. Then she learned of her assignment to the *Vayu* under Commander Singh and bid her former skipper a bittersweet farewell.

And now, despite the date on the calendar, the night was clear and mild, the sky strewn with stars. It might have been Christmastime, but it was still Christmastime in Los Angeles.

The Starr-McGraw ranch in Newhall was literally alight with festive decorations, including electric white Christmas bulbs in swagged strings around the entire main house. Lit wreathes of juniper and holly punctuated the distance between every third swag, making the front look like a very expensive wrapped gift. Automobiles lined the driveway, freshly-waxed and gleaming as if on parade.

The family room was full of party guests in black tie and evening gown, a cross-section of the circles the Starr-McGraw family now moved within. Hollywood actors and directors mingled with aviators and motor sport celebrities of every stripe, along with scientists, explorers, and even a vigilante or two, minus the cape and mask.

While the Edison phonograph blared Annette Hanshaw's recording of *Am I Blue*, "Wings" Jensen chatted with a couple rough-looking stunt men in rented tuxes. They'd been hired on as extra security for the party, but were relaxing until things got "real swingin'". Bootleg alcohol flowed endlessly, as young actress Myrna Loy made small talk with semi-retired western star Bill Hart by the piano. Deadeye was content to keep an eye on Doc from a distance, nursing a non-alcoholic beer. His steady, Kate Shakespeare, was due to arrive the following day on an extended leave of absence from AEGIS field duty, and he was going to make the most of it.

Noted ghost hunter Jim Holland and his psychic partner Mandy Hart chatted near the fireplace with the diminutive actress Mary Pickford, while her husband Douglas Fairbanks talked world travel with occultist Oscar Morgan. More than one stray comment referred to the two men as twins or lookalikes.

Doc waded through the guests, getting grilled from every angle.

"Where's Jack?"

"We were promised an appearance!"

"Where is that handsome man of yours?"

Summoning her prettiest, most hostess-like smile, she nodded and waved away their concerns with promises of his imminent arrival. She knew he'd probably blame their tardiness on Ellen's passion for flying, but also suspected this was his way of making an entrance.

As she found her way through the party crowd to the back patio, she took a moment to admire the floating tea lights in the pool, almost a reflection of the starry, clear night above.

"Where's the man of the hour?"

Doc startled. It was tall, lanky, square-jawed Gary Cooper, moving away from a small group next to the outdoor bar. His chestnut hair was slick with pomade, blue eyes sparkling from a couple of top-shelf gin cocktails.

Doc sighed. "You know him, Coop. After being down with that knee for so long, it's been impossible to keep him out of the Fleetwing." She shot him a wink and chuckled. "And that daughter of ours is a bad influence."

The lilt of the music from inside was drowned out by the low approach of an aircraft, roaring across the walnut orchard and over the back patio. A cheer went up from the crowd assembled by the pool, and a general chatter of "He's here!" followed. The Fleetwing came in from the east, pulled up as it crossed the cliffside, then flipped over in an Immelman loop, throttling down and landing on the north-south gravel runway near the hangar.

Within ten minutes, Jack appeared in the garden, flanked by Ellen and his teenage mechanic, Jinx. "Alright, looks like the party's already started. Go get cleaned up, you two."

Ellen and Jinx took off to the house in a spontaneous foot race, while Jack made his way to the gathered party guests, Doc at the tip of the spear.

"Heya, doll," he grinned, moving in for a kiss.

She turned her head in a mock display of anger, accepting his lips on her cheek, nonetheless. "You knew the party was starting at eight."

"I'm sorry, honey. You know how Ellen is once she's up there," Jack said, reaching for Cooper's hand and shaking it. "Coop, how are ya?"

"Can't complain," the young actor replied. "Although, if you hadn't shown up when you did..."

Jack chuckled at the implied shenanigans. "Say, don't be musclin' in on my dame, see?"

Cooper put up both hands, revealing a highball glass in one of them. "No blood, no foul," he laughed. "Merry Christmas, Jack." He leaned in close to give Doc a soft buss on her cheek. "If you ever get tired of this phony..."

The trio erupted in laughter.

"Aww, Coop," Doc fawned in an overt display of pity. "You're adorable."

"I'm drunk," Cooper admitted as he made his way back to the party. "And I'm gonna get drunker!"

Doc relaxed into Jack's arms, finding his lips for a passionate kiss. "Okay, I forgive you. Best get upstairs and get your tux on."

"Affirmative," he replied, glancing toward the back door, where a familiar face stood watching them.

It was Lucia Flores, her plump, middle-aged frame encased in an attractive satin gown of midnight green. Brunette tresses streaked with silver were braided into a bun, a long string of pearls plunging toward the dress sash. She waved a gloved hand from the back steps, offering a congenial smile.

"Well," said Jack quietly. "If it isn't our friendly neighborhood AEGIS bureau chief."

"She's just here for the party," Doc assured him.

"Really?" Jack asked. "Is she ever *really* just here for the party?"

Doc grabbed Jack by the shoulders of his flight jacket and looked him squarely in the eyes. "Look, mister. It's Christmas and we're not on duty. Your only responsibilities are to keep our guests merry and kiss me lovingly and often. We can save the world after New Year's."

A sly smile crept across Jack's face, and he embraced Doc again. "Affirmative," he repeated, voice low and soft, lips finding hers once more. This time he let himself linger, well aware of the looks from their party guests.

For her part, Doc paid their gaze no heed. When she'd told him to kiss her lovingly, this was precisely what she'd had in mind. She sighed, fully content in the moment.

Finally Jack pulled away to head for the house and his tuxedo, but turned back as if remembering an important detail.

"Oh, uh...Merry Christmas, Doctor Starr."

Doc smiled back, eyes shimmering, bathed in moonlight.

"Merry Christmas, Captain Stratosphere."

The End

ABOUT THE AUTHOR

Todd Downing's love affair with pulp adventure dates back to his consumption of classic radio dramas and comic books as a child in the 1970s, which broadened into a general appreciation for scifi and fantasy media of all kinds.

He grew up in the greater San Francisco Bay Area, writing and drawing from a young age, his works ever-present in school literary journals and newspapers, and eventually on film. He married his high school sweetheart and moved to Seattle in 1991 where he began to write professionally, and worked as an artist in the videogame industry until his publishing company became a full time operation, while raising two children amid the chaos.

As the co-founder and creative director of Deep7 Press, Downing is the primary author and designer of over fifty roleplaying titles, including *Arrowflight, Grimmworld, Airship Daedalus*, and the official *Red Dwarf* RPG. He continues to write genre fiction for stage, film, comics, audio, and adventure gaming products.

Widowed to cancer in 2005, Downing remarried in 2009 and currently lives in a three-generation home in Port Orchard, Washington, with his wife, her mother, their daughter, four cats, and a flock of unruly chickens. Thankfully, he has an office with a door that closes.

Join the author's mailing list:
www.todddowning.com

Thrilling pulp adventure!
www.airshipdaedalus.com

Read the *Airship Daedalus* series:
A Shield Against the Darkness
Assassins of the Lost Kingdom
(By E.J. Blaine)
The Golden City
Legend of the Savage Isle
The Arctic Menace
Raiders of the Red Storm

Plus:
AEGIS Tales

Primordial Soup Kitchen

Calico Kids

The Parish

AVAILABLE NOW
in ebook and print!